The Old West Rides A[gain]

Van Holt

Maben

Ride the Old West

Maben
Copyright © 2013 by Van Holt and Three Knolls Publishing.
All rights reserved. No part of this book may be reproduced in any form or by any means without permission in writing from the publisher,
Three Knolls Publishing • www.3KnollsPub.com

Cover and Book design: KB Graphix & Design • www.kbdesign1.com
First Printing, 2013. Printed in the United States of America.

Chapter 1

The man who called himself John Parker rode into Live Oaks shortly after noon and tied his black horse in front of the Alamo Saloon, glancing briefly along the short crooked street that ran between the log shacks and flat-roofed adobes. He pulled his black hat a little lower over his gray eyes and stepped in through the swing doors and stopped at the front end of the plank bar.

A red-faced, heavyset man standing farther down the bar bared his big teeth in a smile and looked the dark-garbed stranger over with frank curiosity. His eyes lingered on the wide shell belt and walnut-butted Colt pistols in the tied-down holsters. There was no one else in the saloon except the bartender, who set out a bottle and glass when the stranger asked for whiskey.

While Parker sipped his drink in silence, the heavyset man continued to study his somber gray eyes and bleak weathered face. At last he chuckled and said, as though making a joke, "Who was it died, stranger? Somebody close to you?"

Parker's gray eyes narrowed to glittering slits. "About as close as you're standing," he said quietly.

The stout man quit grinning and his face got a little redder.

Parker turned to the bartender. "Can you tell me where I can find an old man named Maben? I understand he lives around here."

The bartender looked uncomfortable and glanced at the stout man, who said, "What did you want to see him about, stranger?"

"I owe him some money."

The stout man laughed. "That's one debt you won't never have to pay, stranger. Old man Maben was found dead at his shack about a week ago."

There was no change on Parker's lean brown face. But he was silent and motionless for so long that the bartender and the red-faced man began to fidget nervously. At last he asked, "How did he die?"

The stout man shrugged. "Somebody shot him. Injuns, like as not. We're always havin' trouble with them red devils around here. Mostly Comanches, but sometimes it's Apaches raidin' over this way from New Mexico and Arizona. He wasn't scalped nor hacked up, so it was prob'ly Apaches. They don't go in for that like them Comanches do."

There was something skeptical, doubting in Parker's silence, in the very blankness of his long hard face, as though he was not quite buying the fat man's story. But when he spoke his tone was quiet and indifferent. "How do I find his place? I guess the least I can do is ride by there."

"It's in the brush about five miles down the valley. You'll know it by the fresh grave. But if I was you I'd make it a short visit. Old Maben just built that old shack on open range, and now that he's dead there's others around here figgerin' to use that land."

"That wouldn't have anything to do with his death, would it?" Parker asked dryly.

The red-faced man looked startled. "Not as far as I know. It sure wasn't none of my boys. I can't speak for nobody else. There's some around here that would do almost anything."

Parker did not appear to be listening. He laid some silver on the bar and strolled outside. The street and the scattered houses were shaded by live oaks and cottonwoods. Even on hot days it should be nice and cool here. This was late fall and there was a bite in the air.

Parker walked past the general store, in front of which stood a buckboard loaded with supplies. On the seat sat two very pretty girls still in their teens. One had yellow hair and blue eyes, the other red hair and dark eyes.

A smiling handsome young man on a sorrel horse had reined in beside the buckboard to talk to them. Now he turned his reckless blue eyes toward Parker.

"Better watch out," the redheaded girl said in a low voice, noticing Parker's guns and his cold eyes. "He's a killer."

She was smiling as she said it and her lovely red mouth was

twisted with mild scorn. Her indifference to Parker was obvious. She had seen two-gun strangers before. They were not uncommon in southwest Texas in the 1870's.

Parker gave her a cool glance and went on by, turning into the restaurant next door to the store. Behind him he heard the young man say, "You could be right. He may be a killer."

While Parker was eating warmed-over steak and potatoes in the restaurant, several riders cantered into town, pulling up before the Alamo Saloon. A few minutes later all five of them tramped into the restaurant and stood glaring at him through mean, hard eyes. They were bearded, ragged, dirty. All wore guns and looked ready to use them.

The apparent leader of the bunch, a big tough-looking man in his thirties, grated, "Hear you been askin' about old man Maben. What's he to you?"

Parker raised his eyes briefly from his food. He had cut the tough steak into small pieces and was now carelessly eating with the fork in his right hand. His left was out of sight under the table. "Was, you mean," he said.

The big man silently nodded, watching him.

"What's it to you?" Parker asked.

"I'm askin' the questions," the big man said nastily. "You better speak up, if you know what's good for you."

"And if I don't?" Parker asked.

"Then I reckon we'll have to beat it out of you."

Parker saw the waitress, a thin pale girl, watching him with worried eyes.

Under the table, his left hand eased a long-barreled revolver from its holster and lifted it above the table. The big man's eyes widened as Parker's thumb cocked the hammer.

One of the other men went for his gun and Parker shot him in the arm, as though casually shooting at a target.

"Anybody else?" Parker asked, watching them through his cold gray eyes.

No one moved or spoke.

Parker deliberately finished his coffee, keeping them covered with the long-barreled .44 in his left hand. Then he got up from the table and said, "Outside. Move."

They moved outside and he followed them. He marched them to a huge old oak at the edge of the street and then said to the big man, "I guess you're pretty handy with your fists, especially when you've got four men to help you."

The big man glared back at him and said nothing.

"You wanted to fight," Parker said. "Let's see you fight that tree. Go on, hit it."

The big man blinked in surprise.

Parker cocked his gun. "I said hit it."

The big man took a deep breath, then hit the oak trunk with his fist.

"Harder!"

The big man hit the tree again, then bent over holding his smashed hand and groaning.

"Any of you other boys like to use your fists?" Parker asked.

None of them said anything, but the man with the bleeding arm shook his head miserably.

Parker heard a horse walking behind him and shot a quick glance over his shoulder. The handsome young man reined in and chuckled at the men standing under the live oak.

"You boys having fun?" he asked.

The big man cussed. "Keep ridin', Billy. We'll get around to you later."

Billy folded both hands on the saddle horn and yawned. "That ain't no way to talk, Dave. I thought we were friends."

"Friends, hell! If you don't leave my girl and my cows alone, I'll make you wish you'd never got born!"

Billy laughed. "You're dreaming, Dave. Molly told me she wouldn't get near you if you were the only man in Texas. And them cows belong to whoever can catch them."

"Like hell! Not when they're on my range! You keep the hell off!"

"You can't have it all, Dave. You'll have to leave a little for the rest of us."

"I'll kill any man tries to take what's mine!"

"It don't look to me like you're in no shape to back up that kind of talk, Dave," Billy said, casually rolling a cigarette. "What happened to your hand?"

"Never you mind! And keep off the Maben place. I'm takin' it over. He was squattin' on my range anyway."

Billy was still smiling as he said, "That why you killed him?"

"It was you, more likely!" Dave retorted.

"You know me better than that, Dave."

"The hell I do! You'd shoot your own mother just to see her kick!"

"You're getting yourself all mixed up, Dave. The way I heard it, it was you who shot your mother, and your pa too. And everybody around here knows I liked old man Maben. You're the one who kept trying to run him off."

"He was on my range, like I said."

"How you figger that, Dave? He was here first."

"Look who's talkin'! You rode in a few months ago and started actin' like the whole country belongs to you!"

"It's all open range, Dave. It belongs to everybody."

"That ain't the way it works around here! A man takes what he needs and holds it if he's man enough! I'm plenty man enough, as you'll find out!"

Dave turned his wild eyes on Parker. "That goes for you too! You were lucky enough to get the drop on us this time, with that sneaky trick you pulled. But the next time we'll be holdin' the guns. If you're smart you'll start ridin' and not let us catch you."

"I think I'll stay a while," Parker said. "I'll be at the Maben place, when you feel lucky."

"It looks like there'll be another grave there before long," Dave said. "That's the only way you'll stay at the Maben place!"

With that he turned his broad back and tramped toward the Alamo Saloon. The other four tramped after him. The chunky fellow stood before the saloon grinning at the spectacle they made. Dave knocked him down, then grabbed his injured hand and howled.

The young man on the sorrel laughed and turned his bright blue eyes to Parker. "That's Dave Shiner and his boys," he said. "You better watch out for them."

Parker eased the hammer down on his gun and slipped it back into the holster. "They better watch out for me," he said.

"You left-handed?" Billy asked curiously.

"I'm left-handed and right-handed."

"So am I," Billy said. He was also wearing two guns, but his had ivory handles. "I'm Billy Brink."

"John Parker."

Billy Brink smiled. "I had a feeling you might be Frank Maben, old man Maben's long lost son. He told me he had a boy he hadn't seen since before the war."

Parker scowled. "What else did he tell you?"

"Not too much. Said he came out here in '63 from Virginia, because he didn't want no part of the war. Said his wife was dead and maybe his son didn't know where he was, if he wasn't killed in the war."

"Maybe he was killed in the war," Parker suggested.

Billy Brink shrugged and flipped his cigarette over the sorrel's head. "Well, I'll mosey along. I promised to catch up with them Baber girls and make sure they get home all right. They shouldn't of come off by theirselves, but their pa and brothers took a herd to Wichita and ain't got back yet."

"They sisters?" Parker asked.

"Cousins. Helen's folks are dead."

"Which one's she?"

"The redhead." Billy grinned. "You can have her. She's too wild even for me."

"I figured that blonde might be pretty wild."

"They're both wild as mustangs. Takes a man to ride them."

Parker changed the subject. "Any idea who killed the old man?"

Billy Brink drew a deep breath. "I couldn't say. But it wasn't Indians. He had some flour and stuff that they would have taken, or scattered all to hell. I've seen places where they raided."

"What about his stock?"

"All he had was a few horses. He told me he sold all his cattle a couple years back. Before that he branded wild cattle out of the brush, like everybody else around here. He had several hands and sold a herd or two every year. Everybody thinks he had money hid around there somewhere, and nearly everybody around here's been out there to look for it. But I don't think they had any luck."

"There any law around here?" Parker asked.

"Every man packs his own in his holster."

"That's what I figured," Parker said. "By the way, who buried the old man?"

"I did." Billy Brink touched his hat and started off on the sorrel. "I'll see you around."

Parker watched him go, then walked back to the saloon to get his horse. Dave Shiner and his men were still inside. The red-faced man stood in front of the saloon rubbing his jaw.

"You lookin' for a job?" he asked Parker.

"Depends on who's hiring."

"I am. Beef Tuggle. I need a man who can handle Dave Shiner and his boys. My men are scared of them."

"Afraid you'll have to do your own fighting," Parker said. "You couldn't afford me."

"What makes you say that?"

"Take my word for it."

Parker untied his black gelding and stepped into the saddle, glancing at the brand on the Shiner horses.

"If you change your mind, ride over to see me," Tuggle said. "Anybody can tell you how to find the Lazy T."

Parker studied him from the saddle. "How many horses did Maben have?"

"Not many. But they were the best in the country." Tuggle grinned. "I guess that's why the Injuns and white horse thieves picked on him. There might still be four or five around there, but you won't find many."

"What brand did he use?" Parker asked.

"The Rockin' Chair. I guess he picked that brand 'cause he was so fond of his rockin' chair. Used to sit out on his porch with his pipe and rock and smoke half the time, after he went out of the cattle business. I think he was sittin' out there when he was shot."

Chapter 2

Parker followed the wagon road south across open prairies, detouring around clumps of brush and trees. The road paralleled Live Oak Creek which was lined with dense thickets of brush overtopped by oaks and cottonwoods. On either side were rocky hills spotted with more brush and stunted oaks and cedars. The cottonwoods were aflame with the colors of autumn. The grass was brown and yellow.

He saw no cattle. If there were any around, they were hidden in the brush along the creek or lying down in the mottes out on the prairie.

The old Maben house was in a clearing in the brush beside the creek. Built of split logs and roofed with planks or clapboards, it was surrounded by tall live oaks and cottonwoods. There was only a small horse corral and saddle shed near the house. The empty cattle pens were out on the open prairie beyond the edge of the brush, which along here was a mile-wide belt choking the valley.

On the front porch there was an old rocking chair. Not far from the porch, under a huge oak tree, there was an unmarked grave that had been covered with rocks to keep the wolves away.

Parker had left his horse back in the brush and approached the place on foot, circling around to the back because he heard the unmistakable sound of someone digging behind the house. The noise of the digging and the murmur of the creek off in the brush hid any sounds he made as he approached, gun in hand.

The digger turned out to be a girl with long dark hair, wearing tight jeans and a man's work shirt. She was digging a hole under the trees at the edge of the brush. Halting behind her, Parker saw that she had already dug several other holes in the hard ground. None of them were very deep. He also saw that she had quite a figure.

"Treasure hunting?" he asked dryly.

She whirled and he found himself gazing into wild green eyes. Her face was almost as brown as that of an Indian, and the high cheekbones and the shape of her nose indicated that she might in fact be part Indian.

She threw the shovel at him, but it only wrapped itself noisily around the trunk of a tree that got in the way. Then she grabbed for a sawed-off, double-barreled shotgun that leaned against another tree closer to her.

Parker cocked his .44. "Leave that scattergun alone! I never shot a woman before. I'd hate to start with you."

She looked at his cold gray eyes and then took her hand off the shotgun, straightening up. She was tall for a girl, only three or four inches under Parker's six feet.

"Move back," Parker said.

She backed up until the brush stopped her, watching Parker warily. He went forward to get the shotgun and looked it over carefully, noticing the initials carved on the walnut stock.

"Are your initials A.M.?" he asked.

"My initials are none of your business," she retorted. "That gun belong to Al Maben. I knew if I didn't get it, somebody else would."

Parker glanced at the hole she had dug, and his thin lips twisted in a wry, bleak smile. "Looks like that's how you feel about his money too."

"That's right." Her green eyes were bitter and defiant.

"What made you think he buried it out here?"

"I've already looked everywhere else."

"Made yourself right at home, I see."

"That's right," she said again. "But after I got through looking in the house, I cleaned up the mess those others made."

"What others?"

"I don't know who all," she said wearily, wiping sweat off her forehead and pushing dark hair away from her green eyes. "Dave Shiner and his men were here earlier, but I don't think they found what they were looking for. I hid in the brush till they left."

Parker eased the hammer down on his pistol and shoved it back into the holster. Then he broke the shotgun open and saw that both barrels were loaded with brass shells. He glanced at the dark-haired girl.

"I reckon I'll keep this. You might shoot the wrong man."

She was studying his face as though seeing him for the first time. "Are you Frank Maben?" she asked.

"I'm John Parker."

"You look a little like Al Maben. You've got his gray eyes."

"How well did you know him?" Parker asked.

She shrugged. "Well enough. I stayed here for a while last spring and took care of him after the Comanches raided the place and shot him. He said if I wanted to stay and keep house for him, I could have his money when he died."

"But you didn't stay," Parker said.

"No, I didn't. I wish now I had. But I figured he might live another fifteen or twenty years, and I'll be lucky if I live that long, the way I'm going."

"Really wild, huh?" Parker said dryly. "Seems like all the girls around here are wild and pretty. Maybe I came to the right place. I like wild pretty girls."

"Don't get any ideas," she said. "I'm Billy Brink's girl."

"Damn," Parker said softly. "The other two I saw were wearing his brand too. But he offered to let me have the redhead. He said she was too wild even for him."

The green eyes were like ice. "You mean Helen Baber?"

Parker nodded. "That's the one."

"That little tramp better stay the hell away from Billy, and that goes for her cousin too."

Parker studied her curiously. "Does Billy know you're here?"

She shook her head. "I wasn't planning to tell him if I found the money. If he gets his hands on it, that will be the last I'll ever see of it. In no time it would all be gone and he wouldn't know what went with it."

"Well, don't let me hinder you," Parker said. He got the shovel and handed it back to her. "I'll let you keep half of what you find."

"I'll bet you would. Unless you're Al Maben's son, you won't get a penny of anything I find."

"Maybe you better not hang around then. There's likely to be trouble, and you could get hurt."

"What kind of trouble?"

"I plan to hang around here a while, and certain folks don't seem to like the idea."

"They'll kill you if you stay here," she said. "They want Al Maben's range and his money and they'll do whatever they have to to get it."

"You mean Dave Shiner and his boys?"

"They're not the only ones, but they're the worst. Half of the thieves and outlaws in this country are their friends."

"What about Billy Brink? How many friends has he got?"

Her white teeth flashed in an unexpected smile. "Everybody likes Billy. Even Dave liked him before they fell out. Billy rode with them for a while, and when he left Dave, three of the others went with him."

"Billy got his own outfit now?"

Her smile faded. "I think they've been hanging around the Baber place. But I imagine old man Baber will run them all off when he and his boys get back from that cattle drive. He don't want anybody messing around with them girls, and the Baber boys are just as bad about that. I think they've been fighting among themselves over Helen."

"Well, when thieves fall out—"

"Everybody in this country's a cattle thief," she said. "Al Maben said he was the only honest cow thief around. He knew the cattle running wild in the brush didn't belong to him. But nobody knows for sure who they belong to, and he never took one that was wearing somebody else's brand, even if he knew the owner was a thief. But he branded all the mavericks he could catch."

"And now you're trying to get your hands on his money," Parker said in a mildly chiding tone. "What does that make you?"

She stiffened with resentment and shot back at him, "What about you? Isn't that what you're after?"

He shrugged. "If I found it, I wouldn't turn it over to any of the thieves around here."

"That's the way I feel."

"It looks like you're a little more greedy and determined than the rest," Parker said, glancing about. "Christ, you've dug holes all over the place. You must have been at it for days. Where's your horse, or have you got one?"

"I turned it loose to graze."

"Looks like you weren't planning to leave anytime soon either."

"Why should I? I've got no place to go, and nobody was using the house."

Parker glanced at her. "Where are your folks?"

"My folks are dead. My mother was a Cherokee girl. But I don't remember much about her. She died a long time ago. My pa was a trapper, but most of the time we were on the move. I was riding before I could walk. The Kiowas killed him when I was fifteen. I've been on my own ever since."

"How old are you now, if you don't mind me asking?"

"Twenty-one, I think. My pa didn't know for sure. He and my mother were living by themselves in the mountains when I was born, and they had lost track of the time. They didn't even know what year it was." Then she asked, "How old are you?"

"Thirty."

"That's how old Al Maben said his son was." She was watching Parker closely. "You really are Frank Maben, aren't you?"

Parker frowned. The question was beginning to annoy him. "You haven't told me your name yet."

"It's Betty Rice." She flushed. "But most people around here call me 'that half-breed' or 'that half-breed Injun girl.' Seems like every time I go to town I hear some old lady hiding behind a window say, 'There goes that half-breed Injun girl again.'"

Her bitterness made him uncomfortable. She seemed to resent him along with everyone else who did not have a natural tan. As a matter of fact, Parker had a trace of Cherokee blood in his own veins. But he saw no point in telling her that. "I think I'll take a look in the house." His lips twisted in a wry half-smile. "That is, if you don't mind."

She shrugged. "Why should I mind? It's not my house." As he started to turn away, she asked, "Did you mean what you said? About letting me keep half of the money if I find it?"

"I always mean what I say," Parker told her. "But you're wasting your time. You'll never find it unless you know where to look."

"It's my time," she said. "And I haven't been doing much else with it lately."

"Suit yourself. But you better stay out of sight if you hear someone coming. There could be trouble."

"I'm used to trouble," she replied. "I've never known much else."

"Same here," Parker said, but without her bitterness. He had found that he did not belong in places where there was no trouble, and found it hard to survive in such places, where there was no demand for his lethal talents. Four years of war had left him unfit for a life of peace.

Taking the shotgun with him, he crossed the yard to the house and entered by the back door. There were four small rooms, one of which had evidently been used as a bunk room for the hands, and another as a storeroom. Besides a supply of grub, the storeroom contained a barrel of water and a wooden bathtub which Al Maben had probably made himself.

In the kitchen there was an old cookstove, a plank table with a plank bench on both sides, a stack of stove wood, and a homemade cupboard. Pots and pans hung from nails driven in the walls.

In the living room there were several chairs, a leather sofa, and a bed where Al Maben must have slept. There was a rock fireplace and another stack of wood beside it. On the mantle a single photograph which showed Albert Maben as a young man with an attractive dark-haired woman beside him. The woman held a baby in her arms, a baby that looked like any other baby.

Parker gazed at the picture with bleak eyes until he heard quiet steps behind him. He turned, frowning. "You move mighty quiet." He noticed that she was wearing moccasins.

She looked at the picture. "You favor them both a little," she said. Evidently she had made up her mind that he was Frank Maben.

Parker glanced at the picture again, still frowning. "You're out of your head. I don't look like either one of them."

She was watching him with shocked, resentful eyes. "You probably aren't Al Maben's son. He would have taught you how to talk and behave around a lady."

Parker glared back at her with his dark brows raised over cold gray eyes. "Remind me to touch my hat the next time you try to empty a scattergun at me."

She flushed. "I guess that wasn't very ladylike. But you startled me. And you looked like a very dangerous man."

"I am," he said and glared into her wide green eyes a moment longer. Then he left her and made another brief tour of the house, pausing in each room to look out the loopholes that served in place of windows. There was only one window big enough for a grown man to crawl through and was in the bunk room. It had neither glass nor shutters, which seemed strange in a dangerous place like this. Parker gazed at it with worried eyes. An unwanted visitor could sneak in through it.

He found the girl in the kitchen, standing near the stove. She turned to look at him with wide, half-frightened eyes. He had done nothing to earn her trust, but was annoyed by her distrust. She was only here because she hoped to find the old man's money, and that annoyed him even more. She had not stayed here and taken care of Maben long enough to earn his money.

She glanced at the shotgun in his hands and said, "I've got a box of shotgun shells out in the brush. I can get them for you if you want me to."

"I wish you would. But I hope you have more luck finding them than you've had finding that money."

"I know where they are," she said and left the house.

Parker stood at the loophole and watched her cross the back yard into the trees. The rounded perfection of her behind, encased in the tight jeans and set off by her slender waist, made him ache with a strange hunger.

When she came back with the box of shells she was also carrying a short buckskin jacket and a pair of saddlebags, fringed and beaded, obviously of Indian manufacture.

"Where's your saddle?" Parker asked as he took the shells from her.

"I left it in the brush. That's the best place for it, if I have to leave in a hurry."

"I think I'll leave mine in the brush too," Parker said. "Both of us may have to leave in a hurry. It might be safer to sleep in the brush. But I'm afraid somebody else might try to move in here. I'm surprised they ain't tried that already."

Betty avoided his eyes. "They may be afraid someone would think they killed Al Maben."

Parker nodded. "Could be."

She was silent a moment, then glanced at him and said, "If you're hungry, I can cook something to eat."

"I'm not. I ate in town. But you can go ahead and cook something if you're hungry."

She looked embarrassed. "I am. I've been here for two days looking for that money, but I was afraid to cook because I didn't know when somebody might ride up. But I guess you can worry about that now."

Parker gave her a sharp look. "What if it's Billy Brink who rides up?"

She flushed and he saw the bitterness in her eyes. "I guess if he finds me here, it will serve him right for hanging around those Baber girls."

Chapter 3

The Baber ranch was back in the rocky cedar hills several miles west of the Maben place. Old Zeke Baber had never been satisfied unless he was on the outer rim of civilization, as far from people as he could get.

He had lost a wife, a son, and most of his horses in a Comanche raid only the year before. Yet he seemed to think nothing of leaving Molly and Helen alone at the ranch while he and his boys and two hired men drove their cattle to the Kansas markets. He would have been far more concerned had he known that the girls were not alone, and that their new-found protector was that smiling young outlaw Billy Brink, who some said had killed a man for every year of his life. If that was the case, his age varied anywhere from seventeen to about twenty-five, depending on who was keeping count. Billy himself modestly claimed that he had dispatched no more than a dozen men, not counting Mexicans and Indians.

Billy helped the girls unload the groceries and unhitch the horses. Then they insisted that he stay for supper. After supper they insisted that he spend the night, saying they were afraid to stay by themselves.

Though almost overcome by their soft glowing eyes and fragrant charms, Billy managed to say weakly, "I ought to get back to camp. I'm afraid them boys will leave them cattle and come looking for me."

"How many cows have you got rounded up, Billy?" Molly asked.

"Not many. Maybe three hundred head."

"Where are you going to drive them?" Helen asked.

"Mexico, I guess. It's closer."

Molly and Helen exchanged a thoughtful glance. When men drove cattle to Mexico, where they were worth only a few dollars a head, the cattle were usually stolen.

"You didn't steal them, did you, Billy?" Molly asked.

Billy looked embarrassed.

"You didn't steal them from us, did you, Billy?" Helen asked.

Billy looked even more embarrassed.

"He stole them from us," Helen said to Molly. "While he's been hanging around here making sheep eyes at us, his pals are rustling Baber cattle like crazy before Uncle Zeke and the boys get back from Wichita and put a stop to their fun."

"Oh, Billy!" Molly wailed.

Billy laughed uncomfortably. "You girls have got the wrong idea. All we're doing is branding a few mavericks."

Molly was suddenly calm. Her soft mouth looked hard. After all, she was Zeke Baber's daughter, impossible as it might seem. "All the same," she said, "I think Helen and I had better ride out and take a look at that herd in the morning."

"Uncle Zeke wouldn't like it if we didn't," Helen said, watching Billy with her mischievous dark eyes. Molly might be concerned about the cattle. Helen was hoping for a little excitement.

"You can still spend the night if you want to," Molly said. When Billy gave her a hopeful glance, she added, "In the bunkhouse."

"Yes, you'll have to sleep in the bunkhouse all by yourself, Billy," Helen said. "It's too bad."

When Billy glanced at her, she winked.

Shortly after supper, Billy Brink retired to the small log bunkhouse, picked a bunk near the door and waited.

He was wide awake when the door opened and Helen whispered, "Billy?"

"Right here," he said.

She closed the door and began taking off her clothes, saying, "I can't stay long. I told Molly I was going to the outhouse."

"You're gonna get us both killed," Billy said. "If old Zeke finds out, he'll be pawing the ground and bellering like an old bull."

Helen giggled, glancing at him in the dark. "Are you afraid of him?"

"I'd hate to have to kill him. Molly would never forgive me."

A moment later Helen was on the bunk beside him, naked and warm and eager. "Forget about Molly. You can have a lot more fun with me."

No light showed at the Maben house in the brush by the creek. The man who called himself John Parker stood at one of the front loopholes, sipping strong black coffee and staring out at the night.

Before dark he had staked his horse in a small opening in the brush. He had shaved and bathed and put on clean clothes from his blanket roll. Betty Rice had washed his dirty clothes and hung them out to dry.

Parker heard the whisper of her moccasins behind him and turned.

"Don't look," she said. "I'm stark naked. I decided to take a bath in the creek and wash my clothes. I didn't have anything else to put on."

"How was the water?" Parker asked, gazing at her dim outline in the dark. The size of her breasts surprised him. The shirt had made her seem almost flat-chested.

"Cold," she said, drying her hair with a towel that she had taken with her. "It's pretty chilly in here too."

"I'd rather not light a fire," Parker said. "You better go to bed and cover up. You can have the bed. I'll bunk in the other room."

"You sure you don't mind?"

"No, I don't mind."

She hung the towel over the back of a chair, removed her moccasins and got into bed just as she was, stark naked. Parker regretted that he could not see her better, regretted it when she pulled the covers up over her long lean body with its intriguing hills and valleys.

"Those bunks aren't very comfortable," she said. "You can sleep on the couch if you want to."

"Maybe I will."

Parker took his cup into the kitchen and came back, saying as he sat down on the couch to take off his boots, "Did you see or hear anything when you were outside?"

"No."

"You could have taken a bath in that tub."

"It was less trouble in the creek. There's a hole down there deep enough to swim in."

Parker smiled. "Next time let me know and I'll go along to stand watch."

"Ha."

Parker put his hat in a chair and stretched out on the couch in his clothes, a gun in his hand. "How is it you're not married?" he asked.

"I was married for a while," she said.

"What happened?"

"My husband picked on the wrong man and got himself killed. He was crazy jealous and tried to pick a fight with every man who looked at me."

"He must have spent most of his time fighting. It would take an awful good man not to look at you."

She was silent.

"I knew that name didn't fit you," Parker said. "What was it before you got married?"

"It was Betty Rice. We were never actually married. We just let on like we were."

"I see."

There was another silence.

At last she said, "I guess you're wondering what kind of girl I am."

"You're my kind of girl," Parker said.

"What makes you say that?" She sounded surprised and puzzled.

"You're here," he said.

"That's only because of the money, and because I didn't have anywhere else to sleep."

"I figure you'd just as soon sleep in the brush."

"Because I'm part Indian, you mean? I'm half white, and I like a nice soft bed the same as any woman does."

"Is that one nice and soft?"

"Yes, it's real comfortable."

"I'll have to try it sometime."

"You can sleep here if you want to. I don't mind sleeping on the couch."

"That's all right." He was silent a moment. "Did old man Maben ever try to sleep with you?"

"He didn't just try," she murmured.

"What?"

"Nothing. I didn't say anything."

"I'll be damned," Parker said, smiling in the dark.

"That was before I met Billy." She sounded embarrassed. "He was lonely and very nice."

"Who? The old man or Billy?"

"The old man. Billy's nice, but I don't think he really gives a damn."

"That was fun, Billy," Helen Baber said as she got dressed in the dark. "We'll have to do it again sometime."

Billy chuckled. "I'll see you in the morning."

"We'll ride out with you to look at the herd," Helen said. "I don't care whose cows you steal, but Molly's got to convince herself that you wouldn't steal from us."

And you've got to convince her that I would, so you can have me all to yourself, Billy thought. But he did not say it out loud, because he wanted to keep both girls eating out of his hand.

He waited a few minutes after Helen had gone back to the main house. Then he sat up and reached for his pants. The girls did not hear him leave.

He found his friends with the cattle, which had been corralled in a pen for the night. That strong pole fence had been erected by old Zeke Baber and his boys, and most of the cattle inside it wore the Baber brand. This presented a problem.

Billy told the other three what they were up against, and added, "Ain't no way in hell we can burn out all them brands before them girls get here in the morning."

"Then we best light a shuck for Mexico tonight," Goat Darby said. When down on his luck he had once herded goats for a time and had been called Goat ever since. But no one called him that to his face except men that he liked or feared, and only a few men fitted either category.

"Them cattle's half wild," Billy said. "Some are a lot more'n half wild. We try moving them at night, we'll lose half of them. I've got a better idea. Listen."

They listened. They always listened to Billy, and the wilder he talked, the harder they listened.

Molly Baber and her cousin Helen slept in the same bed. Sometime around midnight they were awakened by a bloodcurdling panther scream right outside the window. But they knew it was no panther.

"Comanches!" Molly gasped. "We'll be scalped and raped for sure!"

"I hope they rape us first," Helen said. The thought of being thoroughly raped by several lusty savages who knew their business held no horror for her. Losing her pretty red hair was another matter.

The next moment both girls were pulled kicking and screaming from the bed by wild men that they could scarcely see in the dark. Their nightgowns were ripped off. This shocked them but came as no surprise. It was what they had expected. What did surprise them was that they were forced to put on their shoes, which the savages found under the bed and thrust at them, gesturing and grunting emphatically. With a great deal of frantic fumbling the task was accomplished.

The girls were dragged naked from the house and thrown on wild-looking horses, a savage leaping up behind each of them. Then began a nightmare ride that neither of the girls would ever forget. There were only three of the savages and one of them stayed well out in front leading the way. The other two shrieked in the girls' ears, bit their bare necks and shoulders and furiously fondled their breasts while reeling crazily along dim trails though the hills and across the desert beyond.

At last they tired of the sport, shoved the girls off and disappeared in the darkness ahead with hoarse yells.

"How do you like that?" Helen said, looking after the riders in disgust. "They didn't even rape us."

"Just some young bucks having a good time, I guess," Molly said, hugging herself and shivering. Then she said, in a different tone, "I wonder where Billy was when all that screaming and yelling was going on."

"I've got a feeling he snuck off and went back to them cattle before them Injuns got there," Helen said.

"Well, I hope he's all right," Molly said. Her teeth were chattering now. "We better start walking before we freeze to death."

"It ain't that cold," Helen said.

The two naked girls started back the way they believed they had come, stepping carefully to avoid thorns and rocks and hugging their ripe young breasts protectively.

CHAPTER 4

Parker knew he had been asleep when he looked up and saw the shadowy figure standing a little behind him and to his left. Even in the dark he could tell by her outline that it was Betty Rice, if that was her name. He realized that she was still naked.

For a long moment she just stood there peering down at him, not moving or making a sound. Parker too was silent and motionless, except for the pounding of his heart. He wanted to see what she would do.

Realizing that he was awake, she whispered, "I thought I heard something. I didn't call you because I think someone's sneaking around outside and I didn't want them to hear me."

Parker somehow doubted if she had heard anything. He felt sure she had crept up on him in the dark for some other reason. Some sixth sense that never slept had prodded him awake. He was alarmed at the thought of what might have happened if he had not woke up. At the same time he considered other possibilities, even the possibility that she might be telling the truth. Perhaps she had heard something.

He swung his feet to the floor and stood up in the same movement, checking his gun in the dark. "Where did you hear it?"

"I think it was out back," she said, still whispering. "But it could have been an animal moving around back there."

"Won't hurt to take a look. You stay here."

He holstered the pistol and reached for the shotgun leaning against the wall, then felt his way into the kitchen, making no noise in his socks. Peering out through the loophole, he studied the back yard and the edge of the trees beyond. He saw nothing but the trees and brush.

Quietly, he unbarred the door and opened it, but did not outline himself in the opening, nor did he go outside. He softly closed the door and made his way silently back to the front room.

The girl was bent over, hurriedly going through his saddlebags in the dark. She did not hear Parker until he was right behind her. Then she whirled, grabbing for the shotgun. He tossed it onto the couch, then lifted her bodily and threw her onto the bed, falling on top of her and kissing her savagely.

She hissed and fought like a cat, then abruptly threw her arms and legs around him and devoured his face and neck with hot kisses. The struggle continued, but now it was a different kind of struggle. They rolled off the bed onto the floor. There Parker held her and made furious love to her, aroused by her wild and violent passion.

"What were you looking for?" Parker asked in her ear.

"Anything I could find, you bastard!" she retorted, and bit his neck.

Daylight found her spread-eagled on the bed, hands and feet lashed to the bedposts with strips of rawhide.

Parker was at the loophole, blinking his eyes at what he saw. Two naked girls emerged from the brush and came toward the house on foot, hugging their breasts against the morning chill.

Parker shook his head. He had once heard an interesting story about pretty girls running around naked in a dark town late at night. But he had never personally witnessed anything like this before.

"Whole goddamn country's wild and crazy," he said aloud.

Betty Rice lay naked on the bed watching him with resentment in her green eyes, but made no comment. She thought he was talking to himself, which in fact he was.

Parker saw that the visitors were the Baber girls, Molly and her cousin Helen.

He heard Molly say as they approached the door, "I hope no one's here."

"I don't care who's here, so long as they're friendly," Helen replied.

Parker heard them at the door, trying to open it. "Guess it's locked," one of them said.

"Let's try the back," the other one said. "Or the window! We can go in through the window!"

Parker glanced at Betty and saw her watching him as though wondering what he would do.

He stepped to the door, lifted the heavy wooden bar and opened the door. The two naked girls gazed at him with startled eyes.

Molly's lovely mouth twisted in a way he did not like. "Oh, it's you," she said, as though he were the last person on earth that she had wanted to see. She tried to hide her breasts with one arm, her crotch with the other hand.

Helen looked up at him with fascinated dark eyes, making no attempt to hide her beauty. "Hello," she said. "Can we come in? We're nearly froze."

Parker stepped back and opened the door wider, trying to hide a twisted grin. "I never saw so many naked girls at one time in my life. What happened to you two?"

"We were kidnapped by Injuns," Helen said. "But they turned us loose. We tried to find our way back home, but got lost in the dark and ended up here."

She stopped in her tracks and stood gazing at Betty on the bed. "What's she doing here, all tied up like that and naked as—as we are?"

"She tried to rob me," Parker said, closing the door. "I caught her going through my saddlebags and she tried to grab my gun."

"He's lying," Betty said. "He raped me!"

Helen looked at Parker with interest. "Did you?"

"She got what she deserved," Parker said, scowling. "When I caught her going through my things, she turned on me like a wildcat. I had to defend myself."

Helen giggled, but Molly was not amused.

"You're worse than the Indians," Molly told him. "At least they didn't rape us."

Parker deliberately looked her up and down. She flushed, still trying to cover herself with her hands and arms. But he could see her full white breasts. "Why did they let you go?" he asked.

"We don't know," Helen said. "We've been wondering about that. I guess they were just having a little fun, trying to scare the daylights out of us."

"What did they look like?" Parker asked.

"We couldn't tell much about them in the dark. But they were wearing white men's clothes. They probably got them from some settlers they murdered."

"Why would they murder settlers and then turn you girls loose unharmed?" Parker asked in a skeptical tone.

"It's happened before," Betty said. "You never know what an Indian will do."

Parker scowled at her. "Or a half-breed either. I found that out last night."

"Or a white man either!" she retorted. "You wait till Billy Brink finds out about this."

"What's he got to do with it?" Helen asked.

"Billy's my man," Betty said.

"The hell he is!" Helen said. "Billy belongs to me—to Molly and me. Doesn't he, Molly?"

Parker did not miss the icy blue glance Molly shot at her cousin. "It's beginning to look like he belongs to any woman who wants him," she said dryly. She turned to Parker. "If you're through staring at us, do you think you could find some clothes for us to put on? We're half frozen."

"There's some of old man Maben's clothes there in the closet," Betty said.

"If you knew about them, why didn't you put some on instead of parading around here naked last night?" Parker asked.

She flushed and said, "Why didn't you tell me to?"

Parker flushed and said nothing.

"Where are your clothes?" Helen asked Betty.

"I washed them in the creek last night and hung them out back to dry."

"You ain't got any extras? Mr. Maben's clothes will be way too big for Molly and me. He was a tall old man."

"Those I washed are the only ones I've got," Betty said. "So don't get any ideas about them. You'll have to roll up the legs and sleeves of some of old man Maben's clothes."

"I don't want your old clothes anyway," Helen retorted, going to the closet.

Parker started a fire while the Baber girls put on some of Al Maben's clothes, rolling up the shirt sleeves and pants legs as Betty had suggested. Then he went out and brought in the clothes Betty had washed last night. He threw hers on top of her and then cut her loose with his clasp knife.

"Gather up your plunder and ride," he told her. "I want nobody around me I can't trust." Parker had been around too many people he could not trust. But he never stayed around them for long, when he had a choice.

She sat up massaging her wrists. "Why are you letting me go? Is it because of them?" She indicated the two Baber girls warming themselves in front of the fire.

"I just told you why I'm letting you go. I would have let you go last night, but I was afraid you'd sneak back in the dark and try to stick a knife in me."

"You better keep your eyes open tonight, and every night from now on," she said, giving him a look of pure hate. "That goes for you little bitches too. You ain't taking Billy away from me."

"I didn't know there was anything between you and Billy," Molly said. "I heard some talk, but Billy said there wasn't anything to it."

"Billy lied. And he's going to get a piece of my mind when I find him."

"He may be dead," Helen told her. "He was sleeping in our bunkhouse last night, but we didn't hear a sound out of him when them Injuns were howling and dragging me and Molly out of the house. So they may have killed him first."

"How many Indians were there?" Betty asked, putting on her clothes.

"Three's all we saw."

"Are you sure Billy wasn't one of them?" Parker asked. "This sounds to me like a prank cowboys would pull, not the work of Indians."

Molly and Helen looked at each other with shocked eyes.

Betty smiled maliciously. "It was probably Billy and his friends. It would be just like them to pull a stunt like that."

Molly flushed angrily. "I'll bet they did it to keep us from inspecting that herd this morning. I thought there was something fishy about those Indians."

Betty glanced at her. "That's what they've been doing, rounding up your pa's cattle while him and your brothers are away on that trail drive. They already ran off one bunch."

"Why didn't you tell us?" Molly exclaimed.

Betty shrugged into her buckskin jacket and sat down on the edge of the bed to pull on her moccasins. "Why should I? I don't care if they steal all of your cattle."

"She's a thief herself," Parker said.

No one seemed to pay much attention to him.

Molly's mouth twisted with bitterness and she said as though to herself, "Billy can't care much about me if he put us through that last night, on top of stealing our cattle."

"Billy's my man," Betty said proudly. "I could have told you that his dallying with you fillies was only to keep your mind off your cattle."

"That's just what I said last night at supper," Helen said. "But now it seems like a year ago."

Molly looked at Parker. "Are there any horses here that we can use?"

He shook his head. "If there are I ain't seen them. I was told that most of old man Maben's horses had been stolen. Maybe they all were."

"What about yours and Betty's? It's very important that we inspect those cattle before they get all the brands changed."

"You can't have mine," Betty said, picking up her saddlebags. "I've got my orders to ride and that's just what I'm going to do."

Parker scowled at her. "Where are you going?"

"Wouldn't you like to know?"

"She's probably going to warn Billy," Helen said.

"That's just what I'm going to do," Betty retorted. She glanced at Helen. "You want to try to stop me, little girl?"

"Little girl!" Helen exclaimed. "Ask Billy if he thought I was a little girl last night in the bunkhouse!"

"Oh no," Molly said. "You didn't."

Helen nodded defiantly, keeping her eyes on Betty. "Yes, I did!"

Betty's green eyes frosted over and she took a step toward Helen. "You little bitch!"

Helen glanced about for a weapon. Parker stepped between the two girls, facing Betty. "You better go," he said.

"All right, I'm going," she said bitterly. "If you want them instead of me, you can have them for all I care. But you wait till Billy finds out about what you did."

"Don't be surprised if he laughs about it," Parker told her. "I doubt if he cares any more about you than he does about them. Unless I miss my guess, Billy only cares about Billy."

"What do you care about?"

"I care about me. I'm like him in that respect. You're leaving because I don't want you to stick a knife in me some dark night."

"So long," she said, and went out maliciously shaking her hips.

"Can I borrow your horse?" Molly said to Parker. "I want to get to that herd before she can warn Billy."

"Oh, forget about the old cattle," Helen said impatiently. "She already told you it's our cows they're stealing."

"I want to see them with my own eyes," Molly said. "And I want to see the look on Billy's face when I ride up. He won't be expecting me after that business last night. He'll think we're too scared to come now."

"If you were smart you would be," Parker told her. "Maybe he threw that scare into you last night so he wouldn't have to do anything worse."

"He won't bother me," Molly said, "for the simple reason that he's not afraid of my father or anyone else I might tell about what I find. I know exactly what he'll do. He'll try to laugh it off."

Parker frowned. "I think it's a mistake. I don't want anything to happen to you, and I'd hate to lose a good horse, to be blunt about it. I need him."

"Nothing will happen to me or your horse," Molly said. "I promise you that."

"What about me?" Helen asked. "What am I going to do while you're gone?"

"You can stay here," Molly said.

Helen looked at Parker out of big dark eyes. "Do you mind?" she asked sweetly.

Parker was still frowning. "No, I don't mind." To Molly he said, "I'll saddle my horse for you."

Chapter 5

When Parker got to the small grassy clearing in the brush where he had picketed his horse, he found Betty Rice hurriedly cinching her rig on the sleek black gelding. On hearing Parker's angry curse she swung into the saddle and was about to ride off when he grabbed her arm.

She went to her knees on the ground. He grabbed a handful of her long dark hair and yanked her to her feet, slapping her with his other hand. "That's my horse, you bitch! Do you know what they do to horse thieves in this country?"

"Do you know what they do to rapists!" she cried. "You're going to find out before long!"

"Rapists, hell! You wanted that more than I did! You wouldn't let me up!" He shoved her away and stripped her saddle off the black. "Find your own damn horse and leave mine alone!"

She grabbed her saddle and blanket and headed into the brush, saying over her shoulder, "You'll regret this!"

"If you cause me any more trouble, you'll be the one who regrets it!" Parker called after her.

He saddled the gelding and led him through the brush to the front of the house. Molly and Helen came out in their ill-fitting male attire. Parker glanced at them and said, "Both of you better go. The horse can carry double, if you don't push him too hard."

"I'd rather stay here," Helen said quickly. "And I'd just slow Molly down."

"She's right," Molly said, already stepping into the saddle, before Parker could help her. "And when she saw Billy she'd get hot pants and forget what she was there for."

"I wouldn't mind going with you," Parker said. "But if I went there'd probably be trouble."

"I don't want anyone killed," Molly said. "It's better if I go alone."

"Be careful," Parker said. He attempted a wry grin. "And don't get lost again."

To his surprise, Molly smiled. "I won't." She glanced at Helen and said, "You stay out of trouble."

"You too," Helen said sweetly. "When you see Billy, don't forget what you're there for."

Molly flushed and rode off at a fast canter, following a narrow trail through the brush. She was out of sight almost immediately.

Parker looked after her with worried eyes. "She may be headed for trouble. I shouldn't have let her borrow my horse."

Helen looked at him with mocking eyes. "Why did you?"

"For the same reason you wanted me to, so you and I could be alone together," Parker replied.

Helen giggled and Parker picked her up and carried her into the house, putting her down to bar the door.

"I'll bet I can get undressed before you do," she said, already taking off her clothes.

"That's because you've had more practice."

In no time she was on the bed, naked and giggling as she watched him struggle with his clothes.

"Did you really rape that girl?" she asked.

"Do you care?"

"No, I don't care. You can rape me too if you want to."

Parker had to laugh at that, and Helen eagerly joined in with her musical giggle. "I was hoping those Injuns would rape me," she added wickedly. "I wanted to see what it would be like."

"I've got a feeling that was Billy Brink and his friends."

"I know what it's like with Billy," Helen said. "I've been in the hay with him twice already, and all the time Molly was thinking she was his girl. She hasn't even slept with him once yet. I don't think she's ever slept with anyone, and she's almost a year older than me."

Billy Brink and the other three were just saddling up when they saw

Molly coming on the black horse. The cattle were still in the pen.

"It didn't work!" Pod Watson complained, rubbing sleep from his eyes. "We just wasted our time." Then he suddenly grinned. "But it shore was fun."

Molly rode up and reined in, flushed with anger as she looked from the four sheep-eyed rustlers to the cattle in the pen. "You bastard!" she said to Billy. "That was three of you last night, wasn't it? You stayed up ahead so we wouldn't recognize you."

Billy chuckled as he looked her over. "That's a real fine horse you're riding, Molly, but I can't say much for your tailor."

"Those are our cattle in that pen and I want you to let them out!" she demanded. "Right now!"

"We were just about to do that very thing when you rode up, Molly. Turn them out and sort of drift them south a ways for the winter."

"Like all the way to Mexico!" she replied bitterly. "You're just a cheap two-bit rustler! I don't know why I ever let you come near me!"

Hearing rapid hoofbeats behind her, she turned to see Betty Rice gallop out of the brush on the fine dapple gray that Al Maben had given her. The dark girl rode up breathing hard and glanced at Molly with icy hatred.

"I was going to warn you," she said to Billy. "But it looks like I got here too late."

"Looks like it," Billy agreed. "Both of you girls just come from the Maben place?"

"That's right," Molly said. "Helen and I got lost and found her there with that stranger. She was naked as a jaybird."

"I was also tied up on the bed!" Betty retorted. "That cold-eyed bastard raped me."

Billy looked at her with mild interest. "Really?"

"He sure did. Do you aim to let him get away with it?"

"He said she attacked him like a wildcat when he caught her going through his saddlebags, and that was why he had her tied up on the bed," Molly said. "If he raped her, she was asking for it, parading around there naked and trying to steal his money."

Betty reached over and struck her a sharp open-handed blow across the face. "*You're* asking for it, you yellow-haired bitch!"

Crying out with pain and anger, Molly threw her arms around the dark girl and dragged her from the saddle. They both tumbled to the ground, kicking and screaming, and rolled under the nervous horses, fighting like wildcats. The four rustlers gathered around to watch, bright-eyed and grinning.

The two girls were slapping and scratching and biting each other. Molly pulled Betty's hair. Betty grabbed a handful of Molly's old cotton shirt and ripped it open down the front, exposing her full breasts.

"Look at them knockers," cross-eyed Moe Eggert said in a tone of awe, licking his lips. He had stayed with the cattle last night and had never seen those luscious breasts before, not even in the dark.

Billy Brink, afraid the girls would get stepped on by one of the shying horses, pulled them apart. The other three jumped in to help, eager to get their hands on the shapely girls.

Glancing down to see what the rustlers were staring at, Molly saw her naked breasts. Exclaiming angrily, she made a grab for Betty's buckskin jacket, but was held back by strong hands. Betty smiled scornfully at her.

"What we gonna do with them, Billy?" asked Goat Darby, the one who was holding Molly. "If we turn them loose, they'll just be tearin' at each other again."

Billy grinned. "I reckon you and Pod better make sure Molly gets home all right. I'll keep Betty here till you get a piece."

His innocent use of the word "piece" made Goat Darby glance sharply at him. But Billy kept his mild blue eyes on the red-faced Molly, while firmly holding onto Betty with both hands.

Goat Darby and Pod Watson glanced at each other, then hoisted Molly onto the black horse. Goat held the black's reins while Pod led up their own horses. Then, still holding the reins, he swung into the saddle.

As the two rustlers rode off leading Molly's horse, she turned in the saddle and called, "You better stay in Mexico, Billy. My pa will hang you when he gets back."

Billy Brink merely grinned. The man who hung him would have to get the drop on him first, and so far no one had been able to do that.

Helen Baber cooked breakfast and chatted happily while she and Parker ate. He gazed at her in silent wonder. She had been kidnapped by howling men believed to be savage Indians, had been stripped naked and set afoot on the desert on a cold night, and apparently her only regret was that they had not raped her! That would have been a fitting climax to the adventure.

Parker could not convince himself that she was simple-minded or crazy, yet he suspected that there was something wrong with anyone who seemed so eager for reckless thrills and so indifferent to possible consequences.

Leaving her to play with the dishes, he went into the front room with a cup of coffee and stood at the loophole, watching with worried eyes in the direction Molly had gone and telling himself again that he had been a fool to let her go alone. There was no telling what might happen to her.

Helen soon came swaying in from the kitchen and gave him a tantalizing smile. Then he heard the sound of a horse approaching and bent closer to the loophole. Moments later he saw the black horse come out of the brush. The saddle was empty.

"Stay inside," Parker said, handing his cup to the girl. Then he stepped out on the porch, the shotgun at the ready, his sharp gray eyes scanning the wall of brush that bordered the grassy yard. The black horse had stopped in the yard, head high, nervously rolling his dark eyes. Parker spoke to him softly and approached a careful step at a time, still darting sharp glances at the surrounding brush. He got the trailing reins in his left hand and carefully examined the saddle, relieved that he found no bloodstains.

Leading the horse to the porch, he handed the shotgun to Helen, who had come to the door. "You may need this. There's some shells on the mantel. Stay in the house and keep the doors barred till I get back."

He was almost relieved to see the worried look in her eyes. It showed that she was not completely brainless after all. "Where are you going?" she asked.

"To find Molly. I never should have let her go off by herself."

Backtracking the rangy gelding through the brush, Parker found Molly lying naked under a cedar in a little hollow between two low ridges. She seemed to be alone, but he carefully scouted the area on foot before approaching, gun in hand.

Her blue eyes were open and she was lying so still that he at first thought she was dead. There was blood on the ground near her. Then he saw the blue eyes watching him with a strange indifference that bordered on dislike, saw the full white breasts swell as she breathed.

He stopped and stood gazing at her a moment before asking, "Are you all right?"

A hint of wildness came into the still blue eyes. There was anger in her quiet words. "No, I'm not all right. Goat Darby and Pod Watson raped me and rode off grinning about it. I think Billy Brink let it happen on purpose to get even with you for raping that breed girl. She rode up right after I got to the cattle pens and we had a fight. Billy seemed to find it all very amusing, but he separated us and sent those two back with me. He said he'd keep Betty there till they got a 'piece.' That word keeps ringing in my ears. I guess Goat Darby and Pod Watson knew what he meant."

She still had not moved or made any effort to cover herself. Parker saw her torn clothes lying nearby and handed them to her, not looking directly at her. "Put these on," he said. "I'll take you back to the Maben place."

She sat up to put on the ripped shirt. "I've been lying here wanting to die, but now I'm beginning to get mad. I don't blame Goat Darby and Pod Watson as much as I blame Billy. I thought I was almost in love with him. Now I despise him. I hope he gets just what he deserves."

Parker's eyes were bleak. "He will sooner or later. His kind always does." And my kind, he added to himself.

As he was helping Molly into the saddle, the rattle of gunfire broke out in the distance. She looked at Parker with excited eyes and said, "That's coming from the cattle pens. I'll bet Pa and the boys are back from Wichita. Someone must have tipped them off in town and they've caught Billy and them red-handed with our cattle! I hope they kill them all."

"It may not work out that way," Parker told her.

Chapter 6

Goat Darby and Pod Watson got back to the cattle pens on the prairie just as Zeke Baber and his three towheaded boys galloped up from the other direction. The two Baber hands had quit in Wichita, as expected. They were not needed in the winter, and would never be needed on the Baber ranch again.

Zeke Baber was a stern-faced old man with white hair and a straggling white mustache. He glared at the cattle in the pens, and then glared at the four rustlers. Betty Rice, knowing there would be trouble, had disappeared into the brush at sight of the Babers.

"What are you doin' with my cattle?" the rancher cried, almost choking with rage.

Billy Brink laughed openly at the look on the old man's face, and shot him out of the saddle before Zeke could touch a gun. Then Billy turned his ivory-handled Colt on the three red-faced Baber sons and emptied two more saddles before anyone else got off a shot. It was Goat Darby who shot the last Baber son.

Goat went forward to see if any of the Babers were still alive. The boys were all dead, but old Zeke looked up at him with wild pale eyes and tried to draw his gun. Goat kicked the gun away and said, "Me and Pod just raped your girl Molly and left her in the brush. It was mighty good stuff. But don't you worry none, old man. Us old boys will make sure her and that redhead don't get cold and lonesome this winter."

Zeke Baber's eyes glazed over with murderous rage and his mouth worked in a desperate effort to speak. Smiling, Goat Darby raised his gun and shot him between the eyes.

The others were already going through the dead man's pockets and saddlebags.

"Where's the money?" Moe Eggert cried, flinging stuff in every direction. "They just sold a big herd! Must be a goddamn fortune here somewheres!"

Billy Brink held up a thin piece of paper. "This what you're looking for?"

"What's that?" Moe asked, gaping at it in wonder.

"It's a check," Billy said. "That's how he got paid for them cattle."

"A check!" Moe cried as though betrayed.

"Can you cash it?" Goat Darby asked.

"If I can't," Billy said, slipping the check into his shirt pocket, "I reckon I'll just rob the bank that turns it down. But right now we best point them cows toward Mexico and give things a chance to quiet down around here."

Parker had Molly on the black horse in front of him.

"Let's go to the pens and find out what happened," she said.

"Ain't you been through enough for one day?"

"I want to see my father," she said, and then added, "whether he's alive or dead."

By the time they got to the pens, the cattle and the rustlers were gone. Only their victims were left.

"Oh, God," Molly said, staring down with dazed eyes at her dead father and brothers.

Parker helped her down off the horse and watched with bleak eyes as she examined the dead men. He glanced up as a horseman rode into view.

It was Beef Tuggle. The chunky rancher did not seem much surprised at what he saw.

"I guess it's partly my fault," he said, taking off his hat when the girl glanced up at him. "I told your pa in town they'd been stealin' his cattle. Figgered he ought to know. But I never expected nothin' like this to happen."

"You should have," Parker told him. He half suspected that Tuggle was hiding a smile behind his look of remorse. He half suspected that Tuggle had known exactly what would happen.

Tuggle avoided his cold eyes and kept his attention on Molly. "I can see they're buried proper, if you like. My boys will be glad to lend a hand. And I know the wife will want you and Helen to come to the ranch and stay with us a spell."

It had not occurred to Parker that Tuggle might be married. But in a country where there were so few women, he would be just the type to put his brand on the first one he saw, and then watch for a chance to get it on all the others. He would try to go about it in a way that would cause him no trouble, but he would probably get tangled up in his own cleverness, and sooner or later blunder into traps set for others.

Parker saw two of the saddled Baber horses grazing not far away and went to get them. By the time he got back leading the horses, Tuggle had won Molly over with his fake sympathy.

And by the time Parker got back to the Maben house, alone and leading one of the horses for Helen, he was in a bad mood, disgusted and irritable.

Helen came out on the porch and looked at the riderless horse. "Where's Molly?"

Parker briefly told her what had happened, and added, "She went with Tuggle to his ranch and said for you to come on over there. He's going to send his hands back for the bodies. Molly hadn't decided where she wanted them buried."

He saw the shock in Helen's dark eyes. The tragedy had penetrated her blithe disregard for the seriousness of life. "You mean they're all dead? Uncle Zeke and all the boys?"

Parker nodded. "All of them."

"How did Molly take it?"

"Better than I expected. But I'm not sure how she'll be when the shock wears off. You better stick with her. She may need you."

Helen was silent as he helped her into the saddle. Then she looked down at him and asked, "You're not coming with me?"

"I better stick around here. Tuggle said Dave Shiner's been making war talk, and he sent one of his men, the one I winged, to round up some help."

"Ain't he got enough help already?"

Parker shrugged. "Maybe he ain't got a very high opinion of his gun hands. I ain't got a very high opinion of them either."

After Helen was gone, the old Maben house seemed bleak and lonely, and scarcely worth defending. Parker could think of no good reason to remain there. Nobody was paying him to risk his neck. He would soon leave in any case, and after he was gone, it would not matter much to him whether the place fell into the hands of Dave Shiner or some other greedy rancher like Beef Tuggle, or some rustler like Billy Brink. They all wanted the place, and none of them deserved it.

Maybe that was why Parker stayed. He wanted to see men like them get what they deserved for a change. He had seen it happen in other places, had made it happen in a few. Maybe he could pull it off here, even if he did not get rich doing it.

Also, if possible he wanted to find out which one of them had killed Al Maben. He had a personal score to settle with that one.

CHAPTER 7

Taking the shotgun, he scouted around on foot to make sure no one was skulking in the brush near the house. Then he rode down the valley with the shotgun across the saddle in front of him, keeping to old cattle trails where the brush was thick, crossing open places with great care, his eyes slitted and watchful.

In a small meadow near the creek, hidden deep in the brush, he found what he was looking for—four horses wearing The Rocking Chair brand, all geldings. There were two bays, a buckskin and a fine gray with a black mane and tail, turning elsewhere to smutty white.

Parker stayed out of sight in the brush and did not approach the horses, for he did not care to expose himself in the open. Some hidden marksman, expecting him to come looking for the horses, might pick him off with a rifle. He doubted if anyone was around, but there was no point in taking chances. For the time being the horses were better off where they were, and he did not want to frighten them away.

Brushing out his tracks, he returned to the nearest fork in the narrow trail and rode a piece along the other crooked branch, then circled back toward the house, avoiding the route he had used before.

He crossed the creek twice, the second time a hundred yards below the house. Startled by the sudden blasting of guns, he half raised the shotgun, then swung down from the saddle and tied the black in a thicket. Moving cautiously through the brush toward the racket, he stopped when the shooting stopped, then moved on when it commenced again, using the noise to cover any sound he made.

He soon got close enough to see them—two men firing at the house with revolvers. He heard them laughing when they stopped to reload.

"You boys having fun?" he asked in a cold, deadly tone.

They turned and saw him standing there, the shotgun cradled casually in his arm. It did not look half as deadly as the icy glitter in his gray eyes.

Their own guns were empty, and they made no move to use them. Parker thought they looked more embarrassed than frightened. Evidently they thought this was some sort of game. They had a lot to learn. Parker did not play games.

They were both young men in their twenties, with unshaved weatherbeaten faces, wearing the rough clothes of brush riders. Parker had never seen either one of them before.

"You boys working for Dave Shiner?" he asked.

"Yeah, that's right," one of them said, darting a sly glance at the other one, who looked back at him as though surprised.

Parker's eyes narrowed. "In that case," he said, raising and cocking the shotgun.

"Hold on!" the same one cried. His voice was hoarse and unsteady as he added, "We don't work for Shiner. We work for Beef Tuggle. He sent us to bury them Babers, and said for a couple of us to come by here and take a few shots at the house. He said you'd think it was some of Shiner's boys."

Parker's eyes remained cold. "And he thought I'd be gunning for them. He wants to make sure I kill them or they kill me."

"It wasn't our idea," the other one said, carefully putting his gun back in the holster. "We was just follerin' orders."

Parker grunted. "You sure were enjoying it though, till you got caught."

The two men shifted their feet and remained silent, avoiding his eyes.

"Where are you going to bury the Babers?" Parker asked.

"At their ranch. The others are on their way there with them now."

"The Baber girls going to be there?"

"We don't know. Beef didn't say."

Parker eased the hammer down on the shotgun and again cradled it in his arm. "You boys better stick to punching cows," he said. "There's no fun in playing with guns. And Tuggle ain't paying you enough. Tell him to quit trying to be clever. He ain't got enough brains for the job. The next time he sends somebody over here to do some shooting, I'll shoot back, and then I'll come after him. You tell him that."

After the two men were gone, Parker turned the black loose to graze and carried his gear into the house. He ate some cold biscuits and meat left from breakfast, then built a fire and boiled a fresh pot of coffee.

Sipping a cup, he went from loophole to loophole, and considered building a shutter for the exposed window in the bunk room at the front of the house, or walling up the empty hole. But he had seen no scrap lumber about the place, and even if he had any, he would have been reluctant to drop his vigil long enough to use it. Someone might take a shot at him while he was nailing planks over the window hole.

But the window worried him for the rest of the day, and worried him even more when night came. When he was in the bunk room he was afraid someone would sneak up to the window and take a shot at him, and when he was in another part of the house he was afraid someone would sneak in through the window. He hung a blanket over the window, but he knew it would not keep out anyone who wanted to come in.

What he was not expecting was the knock at the back door.

It was almost midnight. He had taken off his boots and stretched out on the couch in the living room, still in his clothes and with a blanket over him because the night was cold. A mournful wind sighed through the brush and rattled the live oaks around the house. When he first heard the sound he thought it might be a limb knocking against the back of the house. Then he realized it was someone knocking on the back door.

He remained still for nearly a minute, listening for any other suspicious sounds. Hearing none, he threw the blanket aside and rose to his feet with a gun in his hand. He glanced at the dull gleam of the shotgun leaning in the corner, then left it where it was, afraid he might bump it against something in the dark. The pistol gripped in his hand, he made his way into the kitchen, as silent in his socks as a dark ghost.

The knocking on the door was resumed. Parker went first to the loophole and looked out, half expecting to find himself staring into the muzzle of a gun, an instant before it exploded in his face. But he saw only the trees moving in the wind and the dark brush encircling the yard. He could not see whoever was at the door.

Turning away from the loophole, he stood against the wall by the door, ready to thumb the hammer of his gun. He knew bullets would not penetrate the squared-log wall, but they would penetrate the plank door. "Who is it?" he asked quietly.

A small tired voice said, "Betty. Can I come in?"

Parker chuckled grimly in the dark. "Where are your friends?"

Her voice changed and he heard the bitterness in it. "You mean Billy and them?"

"Uh-huh," Parker said, darting another quick glance out the loophole.

"They're on their way to Mexico with the cattle they stole. Billy didn't want me to go with them. He said he was afraid I'd run off with some greaser. But that wasn't the real reason. They were planning to shack up with some Mexican girls down there and they didn't want me around to spoil their fun. Billy thinks I'll be waiting for him when he gets back. But I told him to go to hell. I hope I never see him again."

"I thought you wanted him to kill me."

"I'm sorry I said that. After I thought about it, I realized that what happened wasn't your fault. Any other man would have done the same thing."

"It won't work," Parker said, hearing the regret in his tone. He wanted her; it was too bad he could not trust her.

"What do you mean? What won't work?"

"Whatever you're up to. Whatever you came back here for."

"I'm not up to anything. I came back here because I need a place to spend the night. That wind's cold and I think it's going to rain."

"A little rain won't hurt you."

"I'm not as tough as you think. I got pneumonia one time and nearly died." Then she asked in a different tone, "Are those Baber girls still here? Is that why you won't let me come in?"

"They're at Tuggle's place. I guess you know what happened to old man Baber and his boys?"

"Yes. I hid in the brush and saw it all. They never had a chance. I knew what would happen when I saw them coming, and I got away from there."

Parker was silent.

"Hey, it's starting to rain," she said. "Are you going to let me in or not?"

Parker listened. Sure enough, he heard the sleepy whisper of rain on the roof.

"I won't cause any more trouble, if that's what you're worried about," she said.

Parker sighed. People who said they would not cause any more trouble always caused more trouble. And Betty Rice was more trouble than any man could handle, even if he was free from other worries. Unfortunately, she was the sort of trouble few men could resist. Parker doubted if he was among the few. He felt his will weakening.

"Just for the night," he said. "And I'll have to search you."

"I don't mind. I just want to get in out of this cold rain. I got here just in time. It's getting harder."

Parker unbarred the door and opened it, barring it again behind her. She came in bringing her wild exciting fragrance. It was a clean fresh smell. He suspected that she had taken another bath in the icy creek, despite her talk about wanting to get in out of the rain.

Holstering his gun, he relieved her of her saddlebags and laid them aside. "Where's your horse?"

"I turned it loose to graze."

"Saddle?"

"I hid it in the brush."

"Can't be too careful, I guess."

He stood behind her and ran his hands over her from head to toe.

"What are you looking for?" she asked.

"You," he said, and stood against her with his face half buried in her damp hair, cupping her breasts in his hands. "You're a wild one, but I ain't seen many women like you."

After a moment she stirred against him and said in a low voice, "You can sleep with me if you want to."

Parker slept with her. He slept with one arm hooked over her, so that she would not be able to move without awakening him.

The next morning it was still raining, and Parker told her she could stay until the rain stopped. She accepted the offer without comment, perhaps disappointed that it was not of a more permanent nature. Silent and subdued, she cooked breakfast and afterwards moved about the house in her tight jeans, looking for odd jobs to do, perhaps still hoping Parker would change his mind and let her stay. He guessed she was tired of selling her body for a lumpy bed and a meal that she had to cook herself, knowing she would have to leave afterwards.

He guessed also that it was the thought of Al Maben's buried money, and not Parker's irresistible charms, that had drawn her back here. He could scarcely blame her for that. A girl had to think of her future.

She brought him a cup of coffee and said she could keep watch while he drank it. Parker thanked her and sat down on the couch, and she took his place at the loophole, looking out at the gray rainy day. Parker sipped his coffee and admired her backside. He did not offer to lend her a gun. She was dangerous enough without one.

"You see or hear anything of Dave Shiner and his men yesterday?" he asked.

"I heard he was rounding up some of his friends to cause you trouble."

"Where did you hear that?" Parker asked.

"In town. I thought about trying to get a job at the hotel for my meals and a bed to sleep in, or anything they would pay me. But I changed my mind after I saw the way everyone looked at me."

"You sure that ain't just your imagination?"

"It's not just my imagination," she said bitterly. "They looked at me like I was a tramp." After a moment she added, "I guess that's what I am. I've been behaving like one lately."

"What will you do after you leave here?" Parker asked.

"What do you care?" she said in the same bitter tone. "You got what you wanted."

"I was sort of hoping you wanted it too."

She flushed. "I guess I did. That's one reason I came back."

"What was the other reason?"

"I told you. I needed a place to spend the night. I could see it was going to rain."

"You sure it wasn't old man Maben's money you came back after?"

"I wouldn't mind finding it," she admitted. "But I'm beginning to think someone's already found it. I just wish I knew who it was." She shot Parker a quick glance. "It wasn't you, was it?"

"What gave you that idea?"

"I haven't seen you looking for it. So I thought you might have already found it."

"Was that why you were going through my saddlebags?"

She nodded, avoiding his eyes.

"Then I'm afraid you were wasting your time," Parker said. "Which is something I don't intend to do. I'd never waste a minute looking for buried treasure unless I had a pretty good idea where to look."

"You haven't got any idea where it is?" she asked, watching him closely.

Parker shook his head. "None at all."

About midafternoon the rain stopped. Parker, standing at the front loophole, looking out at the dripping brush, was a little disappointed. He had looked forward to another night with Betty.

He said nothing about the let-up in the weather. But she had eyes and ears. He heard her moving around and turned to find her putting on her buckskin jacket.

"You leaving?"

Her eyes were cool and distant. "That's right. It's quit raining and I'm leaving."

"You don't have to rush off. The brush is all wet, and I don't think the rain is done."

Her smooth brown face did not change. She remained beyond his reach. "I don't guess a little rain will hurt me."

Parker studied her thoughtfully. "What made you change your mind? Was it finding out I didn't have the money?"

"I think I know who has got it," she said.

"Who?"

"Dave Shiner. The kind of men he's rounding up don't work for nothing. And he didn't have ten dollars a few days ago."

Parker looked sharply at her. "How do you know he didn't?"

"He wanted to sleep with me and I told him it would cost him ten dollars. Now it will cost him a lot more than that. The price has gone up."

Parker smiled bitterly. "So that's how it is."

Her green eyes were scornful, her mouth hard and a little twisted. "That's how it is. He's got the money, and you're out of luck."

"I think you're making a mistake."

"It won't be the first one I've made."

"I don't think Shiner's got the money," Parker added.

"You're only saying that to keep me here. But you couldn't afford me now. My price has gone up, like I said."

She got her saddlebags and headed for the door, moving her hips in a way that said she knew he was watching. "So long," she said in a sweetly malicious tone.

"Good luck," Parker said. "You'll need it."

After she was gone he slammed the door, rolled his eyes and said, "Women!"

Chapter 8

While it was still light, Parker cooked and ate a tasteless supper, cussing Betty for leaving yet knowing he was better off without her.

About dark, the rain set in again, a slow quiet drizzle that made him regret the necessity of constant vigilance. It would be nice to lay his guns aside and turn in, with no prowling enemies to haunt his sleep. But a man like Parker could never lie down with any certainty that the night would remain quiet and peaceful, could never step outside in the morning without wondering if he would be greeted by a hail of lead from unseen marksmen. He lived every moment with the cold knowledge that it might be his last on earth.

When at last he stretched out on the couch it was with a gun in his hand and only his boots removed. Even then he lay awake listening to every hint of sound in the rainy night.

After a while the rain stopped. It was replaced by a cold damp wind that blew in through the unguarded window in the bunk room, that gaping hole in the wall which was never far from Parker's mind.

It was on his mind when the first shots were fired from the brush behind the house, and he suspected that it was on the minds of the attackers.

He heard the shots exploding like firecrackers at a Fourth of July celebration, heard the bullets thudding into the rear wall, and heard a loud voice shouting, "Come on out, Parker, if you've got the guts!"

Parker, on his feet and checking his gun by feel, was listening in the other direction. He distinctly heard someone step up on the end of the front porch.

In long silent steps he entered the bunk room and stood beside the window, watching the blanket curtain billow in the wind and listening to the man creep across the porch floor. The man thrust the blanket aside with the barrel of a revolver and followed the gun in through the window.

"Come in," Parker said quietly, pressing the muzzle of his .44 to the man's temple. With his other hand he took the man's gun, then prodded him through the dark house to the back door. "Hold your fire!" he called, unbarring the door. "I'm coming out!"

There was a loud raucous laugh out in the brush. "Come ahead!"

The man Parker had captured was smiling. He thought Parker was going to step outside and get himself shot. He had a lot to learn about Parker, and very little time in which to learn it.

Parker opened the door and shoved the man outside. The man threw up his hand and started to yell to those hidden in the brush, but the sound was cut off by the blasting of guns. Parker saw his body jerk as the bullets hit him, saw the man twitch a few times after he fell.

"We got the bastard!" a gloating voice said. "I told Shiner it wouldn't be no trouble!"

Keeping out of sight in the dark house, Parker saw two men emerge from the brush and cross the yard to where the dead man lay. They bent down and he heard them grunt in surprise.

"Hell, it's Leroy!"

They straightened up and saw Parker dimly outlined in the doorway. Perhaps they also saw the dark gleam of the gun in his hand, but if so it did not stop them from jerking up their own guns. Neither got off a shot. Both fell, riddled with bullets that streaked from Parker's blazing gun. He calmly punched the empty shells from the gun and reloaded.

"Don't shoot no more," one of them said. "I'm finished."

"There just the three of you?" Parker asked.

"Yeah. It was Tub's idea. He was always gettin' me and Leroy in trouble. Told Shiner we could get you easy by ourselves."

"How many men's Shiner got now?"

The man groaned softly before replying. "I only saw five or six. But he was expectin' some more. He aims to kill you good."

"Where are your horses?" Parker asked.

"Tied in the brush, down the creek a piece."

"Can you ride?"

The man laughed harshly. "Ride, hell! I can't even breathe!"

He suddenly started coughing and was still coughing when he died.

Parker got their guns and shell belts, then loaded them on their horses and let the horses take them wherever they would. Parker did not really care, so long as it was away from here, and he fired a few shots to send them on their way.

He was not disturbed again that night.

The next morning he tore up the wooden bathtub and nailed the planks over the window in the bunk room, leaving a small loophole which could be closed. No one could get in now without making a lot of noise.

He had just finished this task when Helen Baber rode up on a red and white pinto. She looked fresh and pretty in a full-skirted calico dress that did not seem to interfere with her riding astride like a man.

Parker opened the door and said, "You could get shot riding up like that."

She swung down and tied her horse to a porch post. "What was all the hammering about? I could hear it a mile away."

"I boarded up the window to keep out strays."

She glanced at the window with dim interest and said nothing. Her thoughts were elsewhere.

"Life wasn't exciting enough at the Tuggle ranch?" Parker asked.

"We're back at the Baber ranch. Old lady Tuggle threw us out."

"I guess she caught you in bed with her husband."

"Not me. Molly."

"Molly?" Parker echoed.

Helen nodded. "While the old lady was watching me like a hawk, Molly crawled into bed with Beef. Can you believe that?"

"Not really. It sounds more like something you'd do."

"It wasn't me. It was Molly. She ain't the same after all that business the other day at the cattle pens. It's like she don't care what happens anymore."

"That's a bad attitude," Parker said. "When you don't care what happens, something usually happens that will make you care. But then it's too late."

Helen shrugged as though she had other things on her mind.

"Have you had any trouble yet?"

"Three of Dave Shiner's new men showed up last night. I sent them away."

She looked expectantly at him, but Parker did not add anything.

A smile softened her eyes. She brushed past him and entered the house, glancing over her shoulder at him.

"You can't stay," Parker said.

"Not even for a while?"

Parker relented. "Well, maybe for a little while."

She laughed and began taking off her clothes. Later she lay on the bed naked and watched Parker get dressed.

"Do I have to leave?" she asked.

"Afraid so. There's sure to be more trouble and I don't want you here when it comes."

"I could cook dinner for you before I go."

Parker shook his head. "You've been here too long already."

She pouted as she sat up and reached for her dress. "I thought you'd be glad to see me."

"I am. But I don't want you to get hurt. Come back when the war's over."

"You'll be gone when the war's over."

Parker shot her a quick glance, surprised that she understood him so well. The intuitive knowledge of women often surprised him. But he had hardly expected to encounter any unusual insight in Helen Baber.

After she had ridden off on the pinto, he thought about what she had said, and he knew she was right. He had always ridden on when the trouble was over, and he would again. He could not see himself settling down here or anywhere else. The very thought depressed him. There would always be another beckoning mountain, another distant valley, another town to see.

Even now he wanted to saddle up and start riding. The sun was shining brightly today, the clouds were almost gone, and he hated to remain in the damp and cheerless house. All that kept him inside was the knowledge that a bullet might be waiting for him outside.

Yet he knew that in the long run the house was the most dangerous place for him. They could burn him out, or starve him out, if they did not manage to shoot him. Dave Shiner was not rounding up so many men just to scare him. Evidently the big rancher meant business.

But Parker felt that Shiner would be reluctant to burn the house. Beef Tuggle had called it a shack, but by brush country standards it was almost a mansion, and Shiner might be planning to move into it once he got rid of Parker. It seemed unlikely that he would make such a fuss over open range that he was already free to use.

There was also the possibility that Al Maben's money might be hidden somewhere in the house, and Shiner would not want to risk destroying it. Despite what Betty Rice had said, Parker did not believe Shiner had already found the money. With little doubt, the money was one reason he wanted to gain possession of the place.

For his part, Parker did not believe the money was in the house. If it was, somebody would have already found it. And in fact he thought it possible that somebody had already found it. But not Dave Shiner.

A short time later Parker heard another horse approaching along the trail through the brush. His eyes narrowed with sharp alertness, then blinked in surprise when Molly Baber rode into the yard on a flax-maned sorrel. He opened the door as she dismounted. She was wearing a brown split riding skirt and a man's leather vest that did not conceal the ripeness of her breasts. He had forgotten how yellow her hair was, how large and blue her eyes were.

She tied the horse, then glanced down and smoothed her skirt with her hand as she stepped up on the porch. She seemed different—cool and composed and somehow hard despite the softness of her smooth, tanned cheeks. But she flushed when she looked up and saw Parker watching her.

"I just met Helen on the trail," she said, her lips twisting. "I guess she told you all the latest news."

"We didn't talk much," Parker said idly, closing the door behind her.

Molly's flush deepened as she glanced at the bed. "No, I guess not." She took a folded scrap of white paper from a pocket of her skirt and handed it to him.

"I don't guess she knew about this. I just found out about it myself."

Puzzled, Parker unfolded the piece of paper and read the almost illegible message written on it. *If yu want to cee Bety Rice alive agin bring the mony to my ranch an dont try no fancie tricks Dave Shiner*

Parker scowled. "Where did you get this?"

"One of Shiner's men gave it to me."

"Where did you see him?"

"About a mile from here. He said if I was coming here I could bring it to you and save him the trip."

"Then you were already on your way here?"

The color rose in her cheeks again. She reluctantly nodded, her eyes chilly. "I was looking for Helen. I figured this was where she was. Somebody's got to keep her out of trouble, and now there's no one to do it but me."

"You'll have to get a early start if you aim to keep that girl out of trouble," Parker growled. He again studied the note. "Looks like she ain't the only one who can't stay out of trouble. Betty Rice went to see Shiner because she thought he had the money. Now he's holding her there because he thinks I've got it."

"How do you know that's why she went there?" Molly asked. "Has she been back here?"

Parker nodded. "She came back because she thought I had it. When she found out I didn't, she decided Shiner had it."

Molly watched him through long half-closed lashes. "Was that the only reason she came back?"

Parker's tone was dry. "Can you think of any other reason why she'd come back?"

"Maybe she came back for the same reason Helen did. What do women see in you, Parker?"

Parker shrugged, wryly smiling. "I've often wondered about that myself."

Molly's eyes remained cool. "I won't deny you're rather handsome in a lean, rough way. Your clothes look good on you and you're not bearded and dirty like most of the men around here. But you're hard and cynical and you're certainly no gentleman."

"I've tried being one a few times. But women seemed more interested in me after I quit being one. I don't think women want a gentleman, in spite of what they say."

"What are you going to do about Betty Rice?" Molly asked.

Parker shrugged again. "What can I do? I haven't got the money."

"You don't know where it is?"

"Everybody keeps asking me that. No, I don't know where it is."

"Well, what happens to her is no concern of mine. But I've got a feeling you'll try to save her somehow."

"Do you think she's in any real danger?" Parker asked.

Molly's lips twisted with scorn. "I don't think he'll kill her, if that's what you mean. She's worth more to him alive."

"That's what I was thinking," Parker agreed.

Molly met his eyes. Her own were curious, skeptical. "But maybe you don't like thinking about what else he'll do to her."

Parker scowled. "Why should I care? She got herself in this fix. I told her she was making a mistake."

"There's no reason why you should care. But you do. I think you're afraid she might enjoy what they will do to her."

Parker's eyes narrowed. "They?"

"When Dave Shiner's done with her, he'll probably pass her around among his men. Unless he can get his hands on that money, he won't have anything to pay them with, and he'll have to keep them happy somehow. The kind he's rounding up don't work for nothing."

"That's what Betty said. Maybe she should have thought of— " He broke off, scowling at his own thoughts.

"Maybe she did think of it," Molly said, watching him. "I gather she's not too particular who she sleeps with."

"I gather you're not either," Parker retorted. "Not if you slept with Beef Tuggle!"

Molly flushed. "So Helen told you. I knew she would. She never could keep her mouth shut about anything."

"Why did you do it?" Parker asked, genuinely curious. "You could have any man in this country. Why Beef Tuggle, of all people?"

"He was there."

"That won't wash," Parker said. "You ain't the type. There must have been some other reason."

Her face got even redder. "There was. If I have a child, I don't want to know that its father was Goat Darby or Pod Watson. I'd rather think it was anyone's but theirs."

"You may not have a child. But you're sure to have one if you keep trying."

"Maybe not. Betty Rice has been sleeping around for years and she's never had one."

"Some people are lucky."

Molly was watching him in an odd way. "Would you like to— " She broke off, as though she did not know how to finish.

"I'd like to," Parker said, his face hot. "But not for the reason you've got in mind."

"It was just an idea. I doubt if I could go through with it anyway."

"Only with some clown like Beef Tuggle," Parker said. "You don't care what he thinks of you."

"How did you know?"

"That's usually the reason."

"Is that the reason when women go to bed with you? They don't care what you think of them?"

"Most of the time, I imagine."

"There must be some other reason."

Parker shrugged. The subject made him uncomfortable. He had never expected to find himself discussing such things with Molly Baber. But like Helen had said, Molly had changed. Parker did not think he liked the change. Maybe he had wanted to find one girl who was pure and innocent and beyond his reach.

"I'd better go," she said, catching Parker's embarrassment. "What do you plan to do about the note? Even if you had the money and took it to them, they'd never let you leave there alive."

Parker avoided the question, and asked one of his own. "What about you and Helen? Do you think you'll be safe at the ranch by yourselves?"

She took a deep breath. "I don't think I'll ever feel safe again. But there's nowhere else for us to stay. We tried staying with the Tuggles." She flushed. "That didn't work so well. I'm not going to try staying anywhere else."

"One thing's for sure," Parker said. "You wouldn't be safe here. I asked Helen not to come back till the trouble's over. It might be better if you didn't either."

Molly studied his smooth, hard face thoughtfully. "Do you think you'll be alive when the trouble's over?"

Parker admitted to himself that the odds were not too good. Aloud he said, "I'm gonna try to be. I don't think I'd like the climate in hell, and I doubt if men like me are allowed in the other place."

CHAPTER 9

Parker waited until dark, then saddled the black horse and headed north—toward town. He did not know how to get to the Shiner ranch and he had not wanted to give his intentions away to Molly Baber by asking her. Someone in town should be able to give him directions.

He had cooked and eaten earlier, and he had some meat and bread in his saddlebags in case this took longer than expected. He had an extra pistol tucked in his waistband under a poncho he had donned and the double-barreled shotgun in a scabbard he had found on a saddle in the shed and transferred to his own saddle.

The poncho was not entirely for disguise. A fine Mexican blanket with a slit in the middle for his head, it protected the wearer from cold wind and rain—and Parker thought it would be raining again before long. Toward evening the clouds had reappeared and spread across the entire sky, so that now the night was pitch-dark, the brush and trees shivering in a raw wind.

When the lights of town had begun to wink in the darkness ahead, Parker saw two riders approaching from that direction at an easy trot. He was crossing an open stretch of prairie, no concealment within reach, and he did not change his course. He just pulled his hat a little lower and watched the two riders closely from beneath the brim. He could tell nothing about them and knew they would not be able to tell any more about him.

When they got within pistol range, he called out, "You fellows know where I can find the Shiner ranch?"

"Sure do," one of them replied. "We're on our way there now. You can ride along with us."

"Thanks," Parker said, bending his head to hide his face. He turned the black and fell in on the right side of the two riders, his hand on the gun in his waistband, under the poncho. Out of the corner of his eye he studied the two men. He did not think he had seen them before. "You men work for Shiner?"

"The last few days," the same one said in a relaxed, friendly tone, though there was nothing friendly about his gaunt bearded face. "Rode into town for a drink. Guess you heard he's lookin' for men?"

"Uh-huh. Heard there was some money involved."

The talker grinned. "Sure is. Money and a ranch. Nobody knows for sure how much money, but Shiner thinks it's a lot."

"Sounds big."

"Belonged to an old man named Maben who owned a ranch down the valley. You might of come right by there without knowin' it."

"I passed a dark house. No sign of anyone around."

"Lucky you didn't get shot at. There's a gunslinger named Parker holed up there. Only his name may not be Parker. Shiner thinks he could be old man Maben's son. Anyway, he's the one who's keepin' Shiner from movin' in there and takin' over the ranch and the money."

"Shiner plans to move in there himself?"

"That's the way I understand it. His bunkhouse leaks like a sieve, and the main house is just a shack itself." The man grinned. "But Shiner's got a woman to keep him warm on cold nights. I've seen some women in my time, but I never saw one like her, and it ain't her face I'm talkin' about. She was stayin' with Parker, but now she's at Shiner's place and he's usin' her as bait to trap Parker. Parker don't sound to me like the type who'd fall for a trick like that, and I told Shiner I thought he was wastin' his time. But you can't tell that man nothin'. He's half loco if you ask me.

"Me and Ed has been sort of thinkin' about tryin' for that money by ourselves. But three fellers who tried to get Parker the other night come back across their saddles."

He reined in where the trail forked, pointing. "That's the way to the Maben place. The other fork leads to Shiner's ranch. What say we ride by and see if we can get a shot at Parker, just for the hell of it?"

The other man, a chunky bearded fellow in his thirties, had been watching Parker with a suspicious scowl. Now he spoke for the first time, nodding at Parker. "How do we know he ain't Parker?"

"You don't," Parker said. He had stopped his horse off a little to one side, facing the two men at an angle. "I am Parker. Maybe you'd like to take a shot at me now."

The gaunt bearded outlaw who had done the talking trembled with anger. "You bastard, you tricked us!" he cried, grabbing for the gun in his holster.

Parker blasted him from the saddle, then turned his gun on the heavyset man. The chunky outlaw was leaning forward in his saddle, his head turned toward Parker, his big hand grabbing for his .45. Parker's second shot drew a grunt from him. His third made the man sway out of the saddle and drop to the ground with a heavy thud, losing the gun.

Parker swung down, keeping his gun trained on the two men. When he was sure they were dead, he loaded them on their horses and slapped the horses on the rump, starting them down the trail toward the Shiner ranch. Then he got back in his saddle and followed the two horses at a distance, keeping them in earshot but not in sight.

The trail climbed out of the valley and wound among low rocky hills dotted with oaks and cedars. The stunted trees blew in a damp wind under a gloomy sky. He could barely hear the horses ahead now, but he thought they were keeping to the trail.

Topping a dark ridge, he heard hoarse angry shouts and saw shadowy figures moving about in the vague lamplight leaking from the open door and windows of a shack in the valley below. There was the smudge of a dark bunkhouse and a corral near the lighted shack. Three men had gathered around the two horses and were removing the dead bodies from the saddles with rough hands.

A slender shapely woman in a shirt and jeans stood outlined in the doorway behind them, silently watching.

"You get back inside," the harsh voice of Dave Shiner said, and she stepped back slamming the door. The shapes in the yard looked smaller and darker, staring down at the dead men. "Bastards just had to try it by theirselves, like them other fools! Now I'm as shorthanded as I was, and Doug still ain't got back! Bastard prob'ly won't come back! Well, bury 'em!"

"You mean tonight?" one of the men grumbled, his voice just reaching Parker, who had reined in among some rocks and brush.

"I don't mean next week!" Shiner retorted, and turned to enter the house, shutting the door behind him.

For some moments the other two continued to gaze down at the two bodies. Then, with some grumbling and cussing between them, they lifted the dead men back onto the horses and led the horses away into the darkness. Parker swung down, led the black deeper into the rocks and tied him to a bush. He glanced at the shotgun, then left it in the scabbard, telling himself it would just get in his way. He had rarely used a rifle or shotgun since the war, relying almost entirely on revolvers. Now he checked the loads in the three pistols he was carrying and kept the spare in his hand as he began making his way down the rough slope.

The sound of digging came to him out of the darkness below, but he turned away from the noise and cautiously circled around to the back of the shack. Pausing at the corner, he heard voices inside.

"You better let me go it you know what's good for you," Betty Rice was saying. "You're wasting your time anyway. Parker hasn't got the money, and even if he did have it, he doesn't care what happens to me. Sending those men back like that proves it. That's his way of telling you to go to hell."

"When I go to hell I plan to have some company!" the rancher said savagely.

"You can't keep me here!" she said, her voice rising.

"Who says I can't? I am doin' it!"

"Not anymore. I'm leaving."

"Put them saddlebags down! You ain't goin' nowhere! You'll find it ain't as easy to leave me as it was Parker!"

There was the sound of a struggle inside, accompanied by gasping and grunting and angry cussing.

"Let go of me, you bastard!"

"Like hell! I'll keep you here if I have to tie you up and gag you! Didn't I tell you that was what would happen if you caused any trouble?"

"You wait till Parker finds out about this!"

Shiner snorted. "Let him come here and see what happens!"

Parker moved to the back door and tried the knob, but the door was fastened on the inside. The struggle inside was becoming louder and more violent. The digging continued out in the darkness. Parker went around to the front of the house, making no sound that could be heard above the racket inside.

The front door opened when he turned the knob and pushed. Betty Rice lay half stunned on a dirty unmade bed and Dave Shiner was roughly tying her hands to the iron bedstead. Unaware of Parker moving up behind him, he jerked off his bandanna and gagged her with it.

Parker used the heavy Colt he had borrowed from one of Shiner's men, saving his own guns for more important work. The barrel crushed the high peaked crown of Shiner's hat and rapped him sharply on the head. Parker grabbed the big man as he fell and eased him quietly to the floor.

Grabbing the rawhide rope Shiner had used to tie Betty's hands, Parker quickly tied the man's hands and feet, then gagged him with a strip torn from one of the dirty sheets.

Betty Rice's green eyes were wide and excited and she was trying to speak around the bandanna in her mouth.

"You stay here and be quiet," Parker told her, and to make sure she did so, he left her tied up and gagged, her eyes glittering with wild anger.

Stepping outside with the gun in his hand, he closed the door softly behind him and made his way through a grove of trees toward the sound of the digging. The tree branches rattled in a rising wind and a cold drop of rain stung his cheek.

At the far edge of the grove he stopped against a trunk and watched the two men dig. One used a pick, the other a shovel.

The one with the pick raised up and glared at the sky. "Sonofabitch! It's startin' to rain!"

"You boys better dig a couple more while you're at it," Parker said, watching them with cold eyes.

The two men whirled to stare at him. They saw the gun in his hand, his face hidden by the shadow of the hat pulled low over his eyes. But they knew who he was.

The one with the pick ground his teeth and said, "One of these days, Parker, you won't be holdin' a gun on us."

"What will you do then?" Parker asked.

"You'll find out what we'll do!"

"We?" Parker echoed. "How many of you does it take?"

The two men stared at him with hard eyes and said nothing. Both were big and bearded and in the dark bore a slight resemblance to Dave Shiner. It would be like him to pick men as much like himself as possible.

Parker tucked the gun under the poncho and stepped away from the tree. "This is your chance," he said. "I ain't got a gun in my hand now."

He saw their eyes narrow, saw their muscles tense. The one with the shovel started to throw it. Parker shot him first. He was tired of people throwing shovels at him.

The other one dropped the pick and went for his gun, his eyes now wide with shock and amazement as Parker's Colt swung toward him and roared. He had not seen Parker draw the gun. He knew he was a dead man before the gun flashed crimson, and knew nothing afterward.

Parker left the two men in the graves they had started digging and walked back to the house as a slow drizzle set in. Shiner had regained consciousness and was trying to loosen the rope binding his wrists. He rolled wild eyes toward the door as Parker came in.

Parker took out his clasp knife and cut the rope from Betty's hands, removing the bandanna from her mouth last.

"There are four graves to dig now, Shiner, and you'll have to dig them yourself, when you get those ropes untied," he said to the man on the floor. "But there's no hurry. Those men ain't going anywhere."

Chapter 10

Parker let her saddle her own horse. He waited for her on the ridge, sitting the black in the rain and cussing himself for waiting. He told himself he was every kind of fool there was. But he waited.

At last he saw her coming up the muddy trail on the dapple gray, wearing Dave Shiner's hat to keep her head dry, her dark hair piled up in the high crown.

"Some gentleman you are," she said.

"You wouldn't know a gentleman if you saw one," he retorted. "If I wasn't a damn fool I would have left you tied up down there with Shiner."

"Why didn't you?"

"I'm damned if I know."

"You know all right, you bastard."

After riding beside him a few minutes in silence, she said, "You should have killed him. He'll just round up some more men and it will all start again."

Parker glared at her through the dark drizzle. "First you crawl into bed with him hoping to get your hands on the money. When you found out he didn't have it—"

"I never crawled into bed with him. But if you hadn't showed up when you did, he would have done just what you did that night."

"I don't much blame him! You were asking for it!"

"I've heard that before!"

By the time they got to the Maben house she was soaked from the waist down. The hat and buckskin jacket had protected her above the waist. After taking care of the horses, Parker got a fire going. Betty took off her wet clothes and hung them on the back of the chair in front of the fire. Parker watched her with a mixture of lust and near hatred. She stood with her back to him and he glared at her round behind.

"I ought to strangle you," he said.

She glanced around at him with mocking eyes. "I think you'd like to. But there's something else you want more." She did not have to tell him what that was.

Before Parker could reply, gunshots exploded out in the brush and bullets bit deep into the log wall. Parker blew the lamp out and bumped into the naked woman on his way to the loophole.

"It can't be Shiner this quick, can it?" she whispered.

"I don't think so. There's more than one gun. I imagine it's some of Beef Tuggle's men on their way home from town. This is Saturday night, ain't it?"

"I think so."

"I guess they had a few drinks too many and decided to stop by here for a little more fun, thinking I'd believe it's Shiner's men."

He found the double-barrel shotgun, stuck it through the loophole and cocked both hammers. The guns out in the brush began popping again and he heard someone laugh.

"Maybe they'll think this is funny."

He aimed at the muzzle flashes and fired one barrel and then the other.

Out in the brush somebody howled with pain and somebody else cussed and began firing more rapidly.

Parker quickly reloaded the shotgun and fired both barrels at the flashing gun. There was a hoarse cry and then silence.

"Did you get them all?" Betty asked, so close that she touched him.

"Just sprinkled them good. They'll be picking out buckshot for a while."

"What's that I hear? Is that them leaving?"

"Sounds like it. You might as well go to bed. I imagine the excitement's over for tonight."

"It hasn't even started good yet," she said, putting her arms around him and pressing herself against him.

Parker stood with his back to her, gazing out into the darkness. "Where's Tuggle's place?"

"Why do you want to know?"

"I think I'll ride over in the morning and pay him a little visit."

Tuggle headquarters was several miles down the valley from the Maben place, the unpainted log buildings and pole corrals resembling a small village from a distance. It was midmorning when Parker approached the layout on his rangy black gelding. The rain had stopped before dawn and the sun streamed through a ragged hole in the clouds, drenching the valley in a misty glow.

Parker approached openly but warily, his sharp gray eyes missing nothing. Smoke rose lazily from the stovepipes of both the main house and the cookshack. A man moaned and cussed monotonously in the bunkhouse, and a raucous female voice scolded from the main house, "Ah, shut up! You got just what you deserved!"

Parker drew rein near two men who were repairing a corral fence. One of them gave Parker a narrow uneasy glance, having seen him before. The other one was still in his teens, a big tough kid who had to prove how big and tough he was. There was one in every outfit.

"Tuggle around?" Parker asked.

"Who wants to know?" the kid asked.

"I do," Parker said.

"He ain't here," the bearded hand said, looking embarrassed. "He said he was goin' to town, but I figger he'll swing by the Baber ranch to see them girls."

The kid glanced at the shotgun in Parker's saddle scabbard. "I hear you're purty good with that scattergun. I'd like to see you try usin' it on me."

"I wouldn't waste my buckshot on you," Parker said. "I'd just turn you over my knee and do what your mother should have done."

The older one grinned and the boy flushed angrily, but seemed unable to think of anything else to say.

"Who's that taking on in the bunkhouse?" Parker asked.

The bearded hand looked uncomfortable. "One of the boys ain't feelin' too good."

Just then an angry voice in the bunkhouse said to the groaning man, "Oh, shut up. You ain't no worse off than I am."

"Sounds like two of them ain't feeling too good," Parker said. "And they're going to feel a lot worse the next time they use the Maben house for target practice."

"What makes you think it wasn't Shiner's men?"

"They had a good alibi. And Shiner himself was tied up."

"How do you know he was?"

"Because I tied him up."

The man blinked. "Oh. That kind of tied up."

Parker shifted his weight in the saddle, glancing about. "How many men has Tuggle got working for him now?"

"Just us and them two in the bunkhouse, besides the cook."

Parker's cold eyes went to the bunkhouse. "Then your talky friend came back last night, after I warned you and him not to. I should go in there and put some more buckshot in him."

"I think he had a little too much to drink in town. Them two always start looking for trouble when they get to drinking together."

"They came to the right place, if they were looking for trouble." Parker lifted the reins, glancing from the towheaded kid to the bearded puncher. "If that kid tries a shot at me as I ride off, I'll kill both of you. That's a promise."

The man barely glanced at the sulky boy. "He ain't goin' to try nothin'. If he does, I'll break a post over his head."

Parker nodded and turned the black, keeping his frosty gaze on the boy.

"Anything you want me to tell the boss when he gets back?" the older one asked.

"I'll tell him myself," Parker said. "Looks like he didn't get the message the first time."

Parker rode off at a trot, watching them over his shoulder until he was out of pistol range and then glancing back frequently until he was out of sight.

A fresh set of horse tracks told him which way Beef Tuggle had gone. The rancher had started north toward town, but once out of sight of his ranch house, had swung west into the rocky, cedar-dotted hills. His lips twisting in a wry half smile, Parker put the black into a lope and set off on the rancher's trail. Even if the bearded puncher had not told him, he would have had a pretty good idea where Tuggle was headed.

Parker's slanting shadow appeared before him one moment and faded the next as the sun dimmed behind drifting clouds. His poncho was tied behind the saddle. He wore a short black corduroy jacket and black trousers, his black hat and long-barreled .44s. A dark blue bandanna was knotted about his neck.

Before entering the hills he reined in and looked back across the valley, his eye following the line of the creek with its dark fringe of brush and trees. A chilly shadow fell across his mind like a warning of danger. But he saw no sign of anyone following him, no riders moving anywhere in that wide curving valley.

Turning his bleak, slitted eyes ahead, he studied the big rocks and stunted cedars clinging to the eroded hills and the narrow pass by which Tuggle had evidently entered those hills. A sandstone butte with a talus base overlooked the mouth of the pass, throwing a shadow across the boulder-lined trail below.

A nice spot for an ambush, Parker thought. But Beef Tuggle did not seem to him like the type, and he saw no sign that anyone else had entered the pass since the rain.

After loosening his guns in the holsters, he rode on at a slow trot, his narrow glance studying every rock, every bush, every shadow.

The sound of the horse's hoofs on the rocky ground worried him and he slowed to a walk. He could still see the tracks of Tuggle's horse, as well as old wagon ruts, and he guessed this was the road the Babers used going to town for supplies.

The road twisted along the bottom of the ravine, past more buttes, tumbled rocks and steep rough slopes. It was shadowy and cold. A raw wind blew in his face, bringing the timeless smell of cedars and damp earth.

The ravine curved to the left and climbed between two hills, ending in the sloping yard of a log house. Farther down was a bunkhouse and a pole corral. The yard was shaded by tall pines but swept clean of needles. There were more pines and cedars on the hills, growing among huge rocks.

A saddled bay horse was tied to the rail in front of the porch.

As Parker rode into the yard, Beef Tuggle came out, followed by Molly Baber in a print dress. She flushed at sight of Parker. Parker saw the grinning rancher check to make sure his fly was buttoned. Parker thought he did it deliberately.

"Well, well," Parker said, reining in.

Molly's flush deepened. Her eyes narrowed. She was not pleased to see him at this particular moment. Probably she would not have been too happy to see him at any time. She did not mind letting a fat pig like Beef Tuggle slobber all over her, but Parker made her uneasy.

The thought made Parker sick with disgust and anger.

"Where's Helen?" he asked.

"She went for a ride and hasn't got back yet," Molly said. "I thought she might have come back to see you."

"I didn't see her." He glanced at the rancher, who had stopped near his tied horse. Molly remained on the porch. "I just came from your place, Tuggle."

Tuggle was still grinning, his thumbs hooked in his shell belt under the overhanging belly, short bowlegs spread wide apart. "What did you want to see me about, Parker?"

Parker's eyes were narrowed to icy slits. "To tell you to keep your men the hell away from the Maben place."

Tuggle shrugged. "I already told them. But what they do on their own time is no concern of mine."

"It's going to be your concern the next time it happens, no matter when they do it," Parker told him.

"Let me ask you a question," Molly said to Parker. The marble-like coldness of her face surprised him. "Just what right do you think you've got to tell anyone to stay away from there? Unless you're Al Maben's son, you have no claim at all to that place. And you've as good as denied being his son."

"I think he'd want me to have it," Parker said.

"What you think he'd want is not going to mean much to the people around here," she said.

"It ain't the people around here you're worried about," Parker retorted, and pointed at Tuggle. "It's *him*, of all people. Just look at him!"

Molly kept her chilly gaze on Parker. Tuggle flushed angrily and said, "You got no call to talk that way, Parker. Everybody can't be thirty years old and six feet tall."

"Does your wife know where you are?" Parker asked.

"If you saw my wife, Parker, then I don't know how you can blame me—"

"I didn't see her," Parker said. "Just hearing her was enough. I don't blame you. It's Molly I blame. She should have better taste."

Molly's agitated breasts rose and fell. She was too angry to speak calmly. "If you can't keep a civil tongue in your head, I'll have to ask you to leave. And please don't come here again."

"I won't! I'm afraid I might run into Tuggle!" He turned his withering gaze on the red-faced rancher. "I won't tell you again to keep your men away from the Maben place, Tuggle. You put the idea in their heads the first time you sent them over there to shoot at the house, and if you can't put a stop to it, I will."

"I don't know what you're complainin' about, Parker. Two of my men are in bad shape from all that buckshot you put in them. I was just on my way to town to get the doctor."

"If they're in such bad shape, why did you take the time to swing by here?" Parker asked.

Tuggle darted an uneasy glance at Molly. He seemed unable to think of anything to say.

"So long," Molly said to Parker, her tone now cool and distant. "Don't come back."

He grunted and said to Tuggle as he reined the black around, "Don't forget what I said, Tuggle. It's your last warning."

As he rode out of the yard he heard Molly say to the rancher, "Did you tell your men to shoot at the house?"

"No, of course not," Tuggle said. "I don't know where he got that idea. I figger it was some of Shiner's men."

"Then how did your men get the buckshot in them," Molly asked.

"They said they were just ridin' by there on their way home last night and Parker opened up on them with that scattergun."

And she'll believe him, Parker thought as he rode out of hearing. He was tempted to go back and make Tuggle eat his words. But he knew it would just turn Molly more against him, Parker.

His gray eyes reflecting the bitterness inside him, he followed the road down out of the hills at a rapid trot, paying little attention to his surroundings.

If the kid had been a better shot, or if he had used a rifle, Parker would have been dead. It was a close shave anyway.

Parker heard the bullet whistle past his ear and saw the puff of smoke rise from the stunted cedar on the ledge of a cliff, about twenty feet above the trail. His own gun roared a split second later—he never remembered whipping it from the holster.

The kid's gun dropped first. Then the kid rose on his toes and bent the low cedar sideways as he toppled to the rocky ground below.

He was still conscious when Parker reached him, but there was no fight left in him. His shirt was stained with blood and with little doubt he had broken half a dozen bones when he hit the ground. He looked up with dazed eyes at the tall dark figure standing over him, gun in hand.

"You just had to try your luck, didn't you, kid? You wanted to tell people you killed John Parker, only you weren't going to mention that you bushwhacked me."

The boy's eyes were scared. He knew he was going to die, even if Parker did not put another one in him.

"I could have winged you," Parker said, "but you don't deserve to live. You'd just try to bushwhack someone else. You might have even been fool enough to come after me again."

The boy swallowed. "Gettin' dark. Is it cloudin' up again?"

Parker glanced up at the sky. The clouds were drifting away. "I don't think you need to worry about getting wet." Maybe the boy knew what he meant. Parker did not care.

Parker holstered his gun and went back toward the black horse standing in the trail. "You just take it easy, kid. It won't be long now."

"Don't leave me," the boy said.

Parker did not stop or turn. "I left you a long time ago, boy. You and all your kind." He got the reins and stepped into the saddle. He did not know or care where the boy's horse was. "Don't you worry, boy," he said as he lifted the reins. "Tuggle will be along before long and you can tell him how brave you were. I'm sure he'll be proud of you."

"He'll kick the shit out of me for missin'," the boy said miserably.

"I wouldn't put it past him," Parker agreed. "He's just the type to kick a kid when he's down."

Parker rode off without looking back. The kid watched him go. No mercy, he thought. No damned mercy. But that's what I'd do. Only first I'd get up close and shoot both of his eyes out.

The kid's own eyes became dreamy at the thought of himself riding off, tall and proud, after shooting both of Parker's eyes out. That would have been something to tell folks about.

Chapter 11

Parker found a strange horse in the corral when he got back to the Maben place. It was a gaunt bay with long hair and scars on its flanks where it had been spurred. Parker did not recognize the brand.

He heard voices in the house, Betty Rice's voice and the rough but cheerful voice of a man. Parker listened, surprised and worried. He had never heard her voice sound like that before. It sounded young and happy.

Parker crept up to a loophole to find out what was going on. He saw Betty and a rough-garbed, bearded man engaged in a playful wrestling match on the bed. The man grabbed her in a bear hug. She squealed with delight. They behaved like happy young lovers working up to something serious.

Well, well, Parker thought.

He went around to the front door, opened it and went in. "Having fun?" he asked, dropping his saddlebags and blanket roll on the floor. The shotgun he kept in his right hand. It might prove useful as a club. The young ruffian kissing the girl on the bed looked big and tough as a bear.

The fellow raised a grinning bearded face and said, "Howdy."

"Let me up, Barney," Betty Rice said. She looked flushed but not with embarrassment.

Barney, still grinning, got up off the bed and peered at Parker out of small dark eyes recessed under bushy brows.

Betty sat up on the bed and made some effort to straighten her shirt and jeans. "Parker, this is Barney Hill. He was a friend of my husband."

Barney's grin widened. "Husband, hell. They weren't married. Just shackin' up together, like me and her done atter he got hisself killed."

"She's Billy Brink's girl now," Parker said. "Hasn't she told you?"

Hill glanced at Betty. "No, she never. I just thought she was stayin' here with you."

"That's temporary," Parker said.

"Very temporary," Betty said.

"It better be," Barney Hill said. "You and me's gettin' married this time, so's you can't run off the first chance you get."

"She's bad about that," Parker said.

Hill laughed, showing big white teeth. "Don't I know it!"

"When are we getting married?" Betty asked him.

He scratched his curly dark head. "Soon as we can find a preacher. I don't think there's one in Live Oaks, is there?"

"No, I don't think so," Betty said.

"Ain't you lovebirds forgetting about Billy Brink?" Parker asked.

"The hell with Billy Brink," she said. "I'll teach him not to fool around with them Baber girls and everyone else he sees."

Barney Hill looked worried. "We best not be here when Billy gets back. I could break him in half with my bare hands, but he's mighty slick with them guns."

"There's no hurry," Betty said. "He went to Mexico with a bunch of cattle he stole."

Hill looked relieved. "Well, in that case, we can hang around here for a spell."

"No, you can't," Parker said.

Hill blinked in surprise. "Why not?"

"I don't like your spurs."

Hill glanced down at his long sharp spurs and flushed. "Just try ridin' that jughead without spurs!"

"I wouldn't have a horse that has to be spurred," Parker said. "And I won't have a man around me who spurs a horse the way that one's been spurred."

Hill's face darkened with anger. "Sometimes a man ain't got no choice," he muttered. "It's the horse or him."

"Maybe you should get in a different line of work," Parker suggested. "One that won't bring the posse after you in such a hurry."

"If he goes, I go with him," Betty said. "No one else ever asked me to marry him."

Parker glanced at her. "Maybe you never hung around long enough to give anyone a chance to."

She flushed. "I can remember a few times when I hung around longer than I should have without being married."

"That's all over with," Hill said, taking her hand. She got up from the bed and stood beside him. Looking disdainfully at Parker, she slipped an arm around Hill's waist.

Parker scowled. He had seen about all he could stand in one day. "I've been wondering at the luck I've had with women since I got here. But it seems like the girls around here ain't too particular. Just about anything in pants will do."

Barney Hill took a deep breath. His hands knotted into huge fists. "I hope you got money for a new set of teeth," he said, and swung a murderous right at Parker.

Parker stepped aside and swung the twin barrels of the shogun up against Hill's jaw and ear. Not too hard—he did not want to damage the shotgun.

Hill howled with pain and clapped a hand to his ear, giving Parker a wounded look. "You scared to fight with your fists?"

"I told you he was a gunfighter," Betty said. "Gunfighters don't fight with their fists."

"Can't afford to," Parker said. "What if Billy Brink comes back and finds me with a busted hand?"

Barney Hill spat blood on the floor, poking a dirty finger in his mouth to feel a loose tooth. "You and Billy Brink can kill each other for all I care," he said. "Come on, Betty. We're gettin' outta here."

She kept her eyes on Parker, waiting to see what he would say.

"This makes about the fourth or fifth time you've run off in a week," he said. "That must be a world's record. Don't come back again while I'm here."

"We'll probably come back after you and Billy kill each other, and look for that money," she said. She glanced about the house. "Maybe live here someday."

"You better make sure I'm dead first," Parker told her.

"That won't be long. You don't stand a chance against Billy Brink. Come on, Barney. Let's find a preacher and get married before I change my mind."

She went out shaking her hips. Barney Hill found his hat and followed her, stopping at the door to look back at Parker.

"You forgot something," Parker said. He picked up Betty's saddlebags and tossed them to Hill. Then her buckskin jacket, followed by the hat she had stolen from Dave Shiner. Hill missed the hat and it sailed out through the door past him and landed in the yard near Betty. Parker stared at her rump when she bent down to pick the hat up. That, he told himself, was what he would miss, that magnificent rump. He had never seen another one like it.

After they were gone, Parker found his own company not to his liking. He toughed it out until the next day, then saddled the black horse and headed for town. He told himself that if he saw Betty and she begged him to let her come back, she was just out of luck.

But he did not see her. Evidently she and Barney Hill had not tarried in Live Oaks, en route elsewhere to find a preacher. Couldn't wait to get married.

Parker shook his head in disgust. Women! Even if he lived to be forty he would never understand them.

There were men around who had no intention of letting him live that long, but they did not open up on him at once.

Hoping in spite of himself to catch a glimpse of her, he stopped on the street and stared with bleak eyes at passing women who looked like cows disguised in bonnets and bustles and voluminous skirts. It had always seemed to him that it was the least attractive women who stuck to fashions in clothes that made them look even less attractive.

Parker did not pay much attention to the men on the street. Perhaps he should have. They were paying plenty of attention to him, and none of it was friendly.

He ate in the same restaurant where he had eaten before and exchanged a few words with the thin unhappy waitress who needed a bustle but was not wearing one.

He came back out and Dave Shiner stepped around the corner with a big pistol in his hand and on his shaggy head a dead man's hat that was too small for him. On his rough bearded face was a look of gloating triumph and cold savage rage.

"It looks like I'm holdin' the gun this time, Parker."

"Put that think away, Shiner. You can't shoot a man on the street in broad daylight and get away with it."

"Who says I can't?"

"They'll hunt you down, string you up."

"Who will?"

Parker thought hard. The only name that came to mind was Beef Tuggle. He knew no one else in the country. "Beef Tuggle and his men. He's your real enemy, Shiner, not me. He's just waiting for you and me to kill each other."

Shiner made an impatient gesture with the gun. "You think I don't know that? Tuggle ain't important. I can kill him anytime."

A raucous and somehow familiar female voice squawked, "Who says you can? You put that gun away, Dave Shiner!"

Parker turned his head and saw one of the stout women coming back along the boardwalk, holding up her skirts with one hand and waving the other in the air. She had a hawk nose and a bulldog chin, and she was headed straight for Dave Shiner.

Shiner waved her away with his free hand. "Keep back, old hag. This don't concern you. I'll take care of your husband later."

She kept coming and her voice rose indignantly. "You may scare my husband, Dave Shiner, but you don't scare me! We've had enough of your kind around here! It's gettin' so it ain't safe for a lady on the street because of trash like you!"

She grabbed for his gun and Shiner pushed her away, taking his eyes off Parker for a moment.

Parker saw his chance and whipped out a long-barreled .44. The explosion seemed to jar the whole street. Everyone on it froze to a standstill except Dave Shiner. His eyes rolled out as though trying to see the small dark hole that had appeared between them. Then he fell forward on his face, stiff and dead before he hit the ground.

Tuggle's wife stood gaping down at him in amazement. "You killed him!" she howled. "You're as bad as he was! You must be that awful gunfighter my husband told me about!"

Parker holstered his smoking gun and touched his hat brim. "I'm afraid so, ma'am." He had been taught to respect any old battle-ax who called herself a lady.

Evidently no one had taught Mrs. Tuggle to behave like a lady. She waved her hand and cried, "We don't need your kind around here either! There was too many guns here already! That's the trouble with this country—guns! As long as people carry guns, there's sure to be fightin' and killin'!"

Parker could have told her that in places where people did not carry guns, punks and hoodlums got away with murder. Of course, that sometimes happened where people did carry guns. But all Parker asked was a chance to defend himself.

She did not stop talking long enough for Parker to say anything. She was talking as much for the benefit of the onlookers as for him, and Parker quit listening. He went to his horse, got in the saddle and rode slowly out of town with the angry eyes of the townspeople following him. Everyone was silent except Mrs. Tuggle. Her words still rang in Parker's ears after he could no longer hear her.

He had wanted to kill Tuggle, but now he told himself that anyone who killed her husband would be doing the man a favor. Then he would not have to put up with her anymore.

Chapter 12

Parker felt like getting drunk. But he did not want to go back to town even to pick up a bottle of booze. It was plain he had already worn out his welcome there. Not that anyone had ever welcomed him in that hard-lipped town.

The clouds were gone and it was a warm, sunny afternoon. A good time to be out riding. But Parker was not in the mood for riding. What he wanted was—a woman.

The devil must have heard his prayer. For the one he saw coming was the one he could not have. Don't give up too soon, Parker. Women have been known to change their minds.

She looked good. There was no getting around that. Hair like fine strings of gold, flaming in the sun. Eyes like small pieces of the sky. A rosy brown face that would never wrinkle in a gunfighter's lifetime. Good bones, soft skin. Nice curves.

She was wearing the leather vest, a checked shirt and the split skirt, and riding the flax-maned sorrel.

Her eyes were worried. "Have you seen Helen?"

Parker reined in, scowling. "Seems like every time I see you, you ask me if I've seen Helen. No, I ain't seen Helen. She's probably shacked up with somebody, but it ain't me this time."

She looked past him toward Live Oaks as she spoke. "I'm worried about her. She didn't come back last night, and she said she was only going for a ride when she left yesterday morning. If she's not in town, I don't know where she could be."

"I didn't see any sign of her." Parker thumbed his hat back from his forehead and studied her with bleak eyes. "Tuggle ain't seen her?"

She flushed and avoided his glance. "I haven't seen him since he came to the house yesterday. But I don't think she'd go back to his ranch. Not after—what happened. Mrs. Tuggle would run her off."

"I just saw that old battle-ax in town. She preached me a nice sermon." Parker glanced uneasily over his shoulder. "She may still be preaching for all I know. I got away from there before they started throwing rocks at me."

Molly glanced at him in surprise. "What did she get after you about?"

Parker's weatherbeaten face became even more somber. "I killed Dave Shiner. He pulled a gun and was talking about using it when she showed up. She tried to take the gun away from him and I shot him. Then she turned on me."

"Where were his men?" Molly asked.

"I guess he'd already buried them."

Her eyes widened. "You mean you've already killed them all?"

Parker nodded. "All I saw anyway."

"Good Lord!" she exclaimed softly.

"I don't think Helen's in town," Parker told her, pulling his hat back down over his eyes. "I would have seen her. Everybody turned out to see Dave Shiner stretched out in the dirt and hear what that old battle-ax had to say. Helen wouldn't have missed that, if she'd been in town."

"No, I don't guess so," Molly agreed. "But where could she be!"

Parker shrugged, then asked, "Have you tried following her trail?"

Molly nodded. "I tried yesterday afternoon and then I went back to look for her again this morning. But I didn't have any luck. I'm not much good at that sort of thing."

Parker frowned. "I can take a look if you want me to."

Her face was stiff and cold, her voice the same. "I wish you would. I know I asked you not to come back to the ranch, but Helen may be hurt or in trouble and—"

"Let's go," Parker said, not wanting to hear the rest of it.

When they were almost to the hills, he said, "Take me to where you lost her trail."

"I don't think you'll have much luck finding her tracks," Molly said. "It rained again last night."

Parker shot her a quick glance. "It didn't rain at the Maben place.

Not much anyway. I would have heard it. I'm a light sleeper."

"It rained quite a bit up here. I couldn't find any tracks at all when I went back this morning. That's why I'm so worried."

"Take me there anyway. I might find something."

She led the way along narrow twisting valleys and over rocky ridges, descending finally into a boulder-strewn canyon where she reined in. Parker saw a single set of tracks which she said she had made that morning.

He got down and studied the ground. It was dry and hard. He did not believe it had rained enough here last night to wash out horse tracks. But he could find no other tracks.

He studied Molly Baber with a puzzled frown. "You sure this is the place you came yesterday?"

She nodded, then glanced about the canyon as though seeing a strange place for the first time. "I'm pretty sure. It's awful easy to get lost in these hills and be wrong about where you think you are. I nearly got lost myself this morning."

"Does Helen ride very much by herself?"

"Sometimes she does. But most of the time I've been going with her since we've been by ourselves. Before that one of my brothers usually went with her."

Parker got back on his horse and looked down the canyon. "Where does this canyon lead?"

"Down to the valley. I went all the way to the end of it this morning and didn't find anything. But there are several places where she could have left it. And she's bad at that. When I went with her she was always wanting to try a new route to see what she could find."

"Was there anyplace in particular she liked to go?"

Molly thought for a moment. "I can't think of any. Not when she was with me. There's an old shack about a mile from here where I think they used to go sometimes when one of the boys was with her." The blue eyes brightened with excitement and swung toward Parker. "She might have gone there!"

"Let's take a look."

They left the canyon at a break in the wall and followed a steep rocky trail toward the higher hills, walking the horses. Parker studied the ground as he rode, but saw no recent tracks.

It was almost sundown when they reached the old log cabin under the pines. Parker told Molly to wait with the horses a hundred yards down the trail while he went ahead on foot. Pine needles covered the trail all the way to the cabin door, and Parker felt sure nothing had disturbed the brown carpet of needles for some time except the wind, which was now moaning through the tree tops.

The wind had blown the plank door open. A thick layer of pine needles and dirt had wedged it open. One side of the roof had fallen in, dumping its rotted poles and brush and sod on the floor.

Parker went inside and looked around, then went back outside and beckoned to Molly, who rode on up to the cabin on her sorrel, leading his black.

"Find anything?" she asked.

He shook his head. "She hasn't been here. I'd say nobody's been here in a month or more."

Molly sighed wearily. "We just wasted the trip."

Parker nodded, and glanced at the shack. "Any idea who built this old cabin?"

"I have no idea." She had lost interest in the old shack. "We better start back. It'll be dark soon. If Helen is back by now, I don't want her to start looking for me. I imagine she's been through enough already."

Parker silently mounted his horse and they started back down the trail. The sun was setting behind the hills, its afterglow flaming in the windy pine tops. Darkness was already creeping across the valley below and up the rough slopes to meet them.

Molly's face looked numb with cold, tired and drawn with worry.

"You should have brought a coat," Parker told her.

"I didn't expect to be out this late. Or come up here where it's so cold."

Parker untied the poncho from behind his saddle and handed it to her. "Put this on. It'll keep you from freezing."

It had been dark for some time when they reached the Baber house.

"She still hasn't come back," Molly said as they rode into the yard. "She'd have a light on if she was."

"We'll try again in the morning," Parker said.

Molly gave him a brief glance and swung down from her saddle. "If you want to take care of the horses, I'll go in and fix a bite to eat. The least I can do is offer you a meal."

It was a rather tasty meal. Bacon and beans, hot biscuits and strong black coffee. Parker kept his eyes on his plate and ate in silence, but his thoughts were on the yellow-haired young woman sitting across from him, as silent and ill at ease as he was. He was aware that she watched him covertly throughout the meal.

When he thought of Betty Rice it was without much interest, a fact which surprised him. But he had never been one to pine for women after they were gone or he was gone. Molly Baber was here, very real and warm and glowing in the lamplight.

He said nothing about the food or her cooking. He did not thank her for the meal, feeling that it would only add to the awkwardness. He had not behaved like a gentleman around her and saw no point in starting now. When he had finished eating he rose in silence and got his hat from the peg where he had hung it.

She was still watching him. "You can sleep in the bunkhouse," she said.

He looked at her with a slight frown and left the room with his hat in his hand.

Outside it was cold. The dark pines tossed in the wind. He put his hat on and glanced around slowly, his mind still on the girl.

Later he stood under the pines and watched the lighted window of her bedroom. The curtain was open and he could see her moving around in a white nightgown. He knew she had taken a bath in the kitchen by the stove.

She sat down in front of the bureau and brushed her long yellow hair, her back to the window.

When she laid the brush aside and rose, Parker went around to the front door and knocked.

After a moment he heard the whisper of her feet inside. "Yes?" she said through the closed door. She sounded a little breathless.

"Parker," he said.

The door opened and she stood there in her nightgown, her eyes wide and a little frightened as she gazed at his face.

"Going to be a cold night," Parker said.

She glanced out at the dark pines and shivered, pulling the nightgown tighter around her. "Yes, I'm afraid it is. Do you think you'll need more blankets?"

"I left my blanket roll and saddlebags by the couch. I'd better get them."

She looked startled. "Oh. All right. Come on in."

She stepped back to let him enter and then stood holding the door open, turning her head to watch him.

"You're letting in a lot of cold air," he said.

"Oh, I guess I am." She reluctantly closed the door and looked at him. "I guess the bunkhouse is in a mess. I haven't been in it in ages."

Parker had barely stuck his head in the bunkhouse door, to make sure no bodies were lying around. Old habit of his.

He glanced at the leather sofa, saying nothing.

Molly cleared her throat and said in a low husky voice, "I guess you can sleep on the couch if you like."

Parker said that would be nice.

She barred the door and said, "I'll get you some blankets."

Parker followed her into the bedroom and closed the door softly behind him. She turned and looked at him with wide eyes, a pulse beating in her throat.

"Is this the way it's going to be?" she asked.

Parker took a gun from its holster and handed it to her, butt first. "You can use it if you want to."

"What makes you think I won't?"

Parker made no reply. He unbuckled his gun belt and hung it and his hat on a nail in the wall. Then he sat down in a chair to take off his boots while she watched him over the barrel of his own gun. But she did not use the gun.

"You can keep it under the pillow if it will make you feel better," he told her.

"I think I will."

She went to the bed and put the gun under one of the thick soft pillows, then got under the covers, watching him with her wide eyes.

Parker stood up and piled his clothes in the chair. He blew out the lamp before taking off his trousers. Then he got into bed beside Molly Baber, turning his back to her and pulling up the covers. He knew she was too tired and worried now for what he had in mind, and he was rather tired himself. It had been a long day.

"Go to sleep," he said.

She remained silent until he was half asleep. Then she said, "Parker, do you think you can find her?"

"We'll find her," he said. "Go to sleep."

The sound of the wind in the pines was the last thing he heard before he went to sleep. He heard it still blowing hours later when he woke up.

"Parker," she said, "are you awake?"

He turned toward her and she came willingly into his arms, wanting him as much as he wanted her.

Later she asked, "Why did you give me the gun? That was taking a chance. I might have used it."

"I unloaded it before I came in."

"I should have known. Then it was just a trick. I should be angry, but I'm not."

"Don't you have any guns here?" Parker asked. "I didn't see any."

"Helen hid them all. I think she was afraid I might shoot Billy Brink if he ever comes back here. Or even that I might shoot myself."

"Did you think about shooting yourself?"

"Once or twice."

"Do you still think about it?"

"Sometimes."

Parker was silent.

"I just thought of something," Molly said in a different tone. "Helen took her saddlebags with her. She never did that before when she went for a ride. And she was wearing her jacket. She usually goes off in any kind of weather without one. Do you think she was planning to leave?"

"Wouldn't she have told you?"

"She might not have. We had an argument the night before." Molly sat up suddenly. "I'll bet I know where she's gone."

"Where?"

"To meet Billy Brink. I think she's half in love with him. And I told her I'd never allow him to come back here."

"Was that what the argument was about? Billy Brink?"

"Yes. We said some pretty nasty things to each other. Each of us accused the other of being in love with him. Things like that."

"Why didn't you tell me this before?" Parker asked with a trace of irritation.

"I didn't think it concerned anyone but me and Helen. And I guess I couldn't bring myself to believe she'd leave without telling me, much less that she'd head for the border to meet Billy. But I'll bet that's just what she did."

"Do you think they'll be coming back already?"

"I look for them to show up anytime. I'm sure they didn't waste any time on the way down there with those stolen cattle. And Billy won't stay down there long, the way he left things around here. He doesn't want people to think he's afraid to come back, or that he's afraid of you."

Chapter 13

Parker got the empty gun from under the pillow and rose from the bed. He got dressed in the dark, buckled on his shell belt, then loaded the gun.

"Are you leaving?" Molly asked.

"I'll be around."

"I'm not in love with Billy Brink," she said.

"I didn't ask."

"What's wrong then?"

"Everything. I don't mind being lied to a little, but you overdid it. You knew where Helen was all the time. And she didn't leave when you said she did. It hasn't rained since then. She left before the rain."

"Beef Tuggle was here when I told you that. I thought it would take too much explaining if I said she'd left the day before. It seemed simpler just to say she'd gone for a ride. And later I hated to change my story."

"So you dragged me all over those hills looking for her, when you knew all the time she was on her way to meet Billy Brink." He holstered the gun, smiling grimly in the dark. "I thought I was being clever with that gun trick, but you were way ahead of me. You had the whole thing planned. You wanted her and Billy to find me here with you, wanted to show them both you didn't care what they did. I don't like being used that way, lady."

"It's not like that." After a moment she added, "I wanted you to kill him."

Parker stared at her, but it was too dark to tell anything about her face.

"Either way, you were using me, and I don't like being used."

As he went out into the cold windy night, carrying his saddlebags and blanket roll and the sawed-off shotgun, it occurred to him that she was still using him. For he could not leave until he knew she was safe.

Shortly after daylight three men and a girl rode into the Baber yard on tired horses. Goat Darby, Pod Watson, Moe Eggert and Helen Baber.

Billy Brink was not with them.

Molly Baber stepped out on the porch in a warm coat. Her blue eyes were like ice. "Don't bother to get down. You're not wanted here."

Helen Baber smiled. "Does that include me, Molly?"

Molly's eyes softened a little as she looked at her lovely red-haired cousin. "Are you all right? I've been worried to death."

"What were you worried about?" Helen asked sweetly as she swung down from the saddle. "Were you afraid Billy and me were using the same blankets?"

Molly's eyes frosted over again. "It looks like he didn't enjoy it too much. I see he didn't come back with you."

"I think it was you he didn't want to see," Helen said in the same innocent tone. "But he may come up later. He said he had some things to do down in the valley."

Grinning, the three dirty, unshaved rustlers were about to dismount when Parker stepped around the corner of the house, his thumbs hooked carelessly in his shell belt, his guns in the tied-down holsters. His bleak gray eyes were a few degrees colder than Molly Baber's.

"I believe the lady said you boys weren't wanted here."

Moe Eggert bared his crooked yellow teeth in a grin, his cross eyes gleaming. "Not bein' wanted never stopped us before."

"It will this time."

"You don't say." Eggert's hairy right hand moved toward his holstered gun. It was not clear whether he meant to draw the gun or was just getting ready to draw if a fight started. Parker did not wait to find out. A man could get killed that way.

He shot Moe Eggert off his horse.

Goat Darby and Pod Watson sat frozen in their saddles, staring at the smoking gun with shocked eyes. They had not seen Parker draw the gun from the holster, although their eyes had not left him since he stepped around the corner of the house.

"Start riding," Parker said. "And take him with you."

Pod Watson quickly got down and slung the dead man across his saddle, then got back on his horse. Goat Darby had not moved or taken his dark eyes off Parker. But now he glanced at Molly Baber and his eyes strayed over her body.

"Kill them!" she cried, trembling with cold fury at the memory of what they had done to her. "Or give me the gun and I will!"

Parker did not look at her. "Start riding," he said again to the two rustlers. They still had their guns. If they wanted to use them, that was fine with him.

They turned their horses and started out of the yard, Pod Watson leading Moe Eggert's horse.

"They'll be back," Molly said bitterly.

"They won't be back," Parker said.

Goat Darby glanced back at him with scornful eyes.

Helen Baber stood near the bottom step, smiling at Parker as though nothing had happened. He remembered his first impression of her—that she was a silly, empty-headed girl.

"Hi, Parker," she said.

"Get inside," he said. "Both of you. Get inside and stay there. It's not over."

"What about my horse?" Helen asked, glancing at the pinto.

"Worry about the horse later."

"Whatever you say, Parker."

She climbed the steps and walked past Molly into the house.

About to turn, Molly gave Parker a faint smile and said, "Thanks for calling me a lady. I know I don't deserve it, but it sounded good."

"It was just a word," Parker said, looking after the rustlers.

Molly nodded and followed Helen into the house, closing the door behind her.

The rustlers were soon out of sight. Parker could no longer hear their horses. He walked to the edge of the yard where he could see the curving trail below. He saw Darby and Watson dismount and check their guns. They left the three horses standing in the road and began making their way up the slope through the rocks and trees toward the house. They did not see Parker.

When they were halfway up the slope, he stepped out from behind a rock twenty feet to their left, a long-barreled .44 in his hand.

"Drop the guns or I'll drop you."

They dived for cover, firing as they dived. Parker shot Darby through the body. The rustler turned over in the air and landed with a loud grunt, but managed to scramble behind a rock. Watson was already out of sight.

Parker stepped behind the rock, punched out the empty shell and thumbed in a fresh one from his belt. He had already replaced the cartridge fired at Moe Eggert, and added a sixth cartridge in the chamber normally left empty. Now he had two fully loaded pistols, the ones he knew and relied on. He had not brought the shotgun.

He heard one of them circling through the rocks to flank him. That would be Watson. Bent low, Parker began moving to his right, his boots making no sound on the carpet of pine needles. He was not wearing spurs.

He waited behind a thick pine trunk, turned sideways to lessen the risk of being seen, and soon heard quiet steps approaching.

He stepped out and fired just as the wild-eyed rustler flung a hasty shot at him. Watson's bullet knocked bark from the tree a foot above Parker's head. Parker's bullet knocked dust from Watson's ragged wool coat.

Watson coughed and fell, shuddered and died.

Parker picked up the man's gun and fired at the tree where he himself had been standing, waited a few minutes and fired again. That would give the wounded Goat Darby something to wonder about.

Darby yelled with a sudden impatience, "Hurry up and kill the bastard, Pod, before I bleed to death!"

You won't ever live that long, Parker thought.

He fired two quick shots at the tree and put Watson's empty gun down.

"Get 'im?" Darby called.

Yeah, I got 'im, Parker thought, replacing the empty shell in his .44 with a live round.

He looked about and then went back the way he had come, circling around behind the wounded man, who would be watching in the direction Pod Watson had gone.

"Pod!" Darby yelled, raising himself up to peer downslope.

"He can't hear you," Parker said behind him.

Despite the cold, Darby had taken off his hat, coat and shirt, and had torn the dirty shirt into strips to bandage the wound in his hairy chest. The bandage was soaked with blood and it seemed a miracle that he was still alive.

He twisted around to fire. But Parker had moved again, was standing behind a low rock several feet from where he had spoken, with a gun in each hand. He fired the gun in his right hand and then the one in his left. The first bullet flung Darby back against a boulder. The second entered just below his right eye.

Parker carried him down the hill and loaded him on one of the horses, then went back to get Watson.

Helen Baber was bending over the dead rustler. She straightened up with Watson's gun in her hand.

"I told you to stay in the house," Parker said.

She pointed the gun at him, smiling. "I don't want you to kill Billy." She cocked the hammer and pulled the trigger. The gun clicked on an empty chamber.

"I knew it wasn't loaded," she said with apparent unconcern, and tossed the gun aside.

Parker took two long steps and back-handed her across the face, knocking her to the ground on her butt. "You're a cute little trick of a girl," he said. "But you've got the morals of an alley cat and the brains of a monkey, and if I see you again before I leave I'll turn you over my knee and spank some sense into that empty little head of yours. Now get out of my sight."

Wasting no more time with her, he carried Watson's body down, lashed all three rustlers securely across their saddles and slapped the horses on the rump to send them down the trial. Let the fine folks of the valley bury the rustlers when they found the horses grazing on their range. Parker had done his part.

He went back up the hill to saddle his horse. He was tightening the cinch when Molly Baber appeared.

"I sent the rustlers away on their horses. I didn't figure you wanted them buried around here."

"No, I didn't." She watched him a moment in silence. Parker kept his back to her. "Are you coming back?"

"No."

She sighed.

"Don't worry," Parker said. "I'm sure Tuggle will be dropping by."

Her eyes narrowed. "I figured you'd kill him too."

"I'm afraid I'd be doing him a favor if I killed him."

"You mean because of me?"

"Partly. But mainly because of that old battle-ax he's married to."

When Parker was in the saddle, she asked, "What about Billy Brink? Will he be dropping by too?"

"I doubt it."

"I hope not," she said, her tone cool and distant.

Parker nodded without looking at her and started the black horse down the trail toward the valley. He did not look back.

He tied the horse in the brush near the Maben house. He could hear someone digging in the front yard. He was a little disappointed when he saw that it was not Betty Rice. He had half hoped to see her again before he left.

It was Billy Brink and he was digging up Al Maben's grave. He looked up with a grin when Parker stepped out of the brush. He seemed glad to see the tall somber man in black.

"Is that where you buried it?" Parker asked.

Billy nodded. "I didn't figger anyone would think to look for it in his grave. Seemed like a good place to leave it for a while."

"Did you kill him for the money?" Parker asked.

"That was the main reason," Billy admitted. "I sort of liked him, but he never trusted me. If he had—"

"You would have killed him anyway," Parker said.

"Maybe." Billy put the shovel down and stepped out of the grave. He glanced down at his hands. "I should have waited till later about that digging."

"A gunfighter has to take care of his hands," Parker agreed. "You should know that by now."

Billy shrugged. "I don't guess shoveling a little loose dirt should hurt too much. I didn't bury it very deep. Knew I'd soon be coming back for it."

Parker said nothing. He waited.

Billy grinned. "Too bad we're all alone. A lot of folks around here have been looking forward to seeing this."

"Too bad," Parker agreed, still somber and remote.

"Say when," Billy Brink said.

"When."

Billy Brink's hand streaked toward his gun. He had the gun half out of the holster when Parker's bullet killed him. The young outlaw fell to the ground only a few feet from Al Maben's grave.

Parker walked slowly to the grave, scarcely glancing at the dead youth, who no longer mattered. He stared down into the grave.

"Is this what you wanted, old man?"

What did Parker himself want? What had the boy named Frank Maben wanted? Perhaps it did not matter, for he had never found it. And the man who called himself John Parker had never found what he wanted either. After ten years of searching since the war he was no closer to it than when he had started.

But he knew he would never stop looking. Even now the unknown places were calling to him. Maybe somewhere, in some remote valley or some strange town, he would find whatever he was looking for.

Thank you for reading
Maben
by Van Holt.

We hope you enjoyed this story. If so, please leave a review about your experience on Amazon so others may discover Van Holt.

You may also enjoy another story about some famous gunfighters called *The Hellbound Man*.

Excerpt from
The Hellbound Man
by Van Holt

Jim Benton was riding another lonely trail which he knew would soon lead him to more trouble, if it led anywhere. But it did not really matter. He was past thirty and past caring. He had already lived longer than he had expected to.

He wore dark clothes and rode a dark horse. The horse was dark brown but most people would have called it a black horse. Benton's hair was dark brown with a copper or reddish tinge, but most people would have said it was black, and under the frowning dark brows his gray eyes often looked black too. Whatever Benton wore looked black on him. But he never wore light-colored clothes. They were too easily seen, made too good a target.

He was a tall lean man with a strength in his arms and shoulders that was not apparent at first glance. But there were taller and stronger men, and somewhere there was a man who was faster with a gun, or one who would put a bullet in his back. Every step along the trail brought him that much closer to such a man. But he could not stop and he could not turn back. He had to keep going.

A barren desert waste lay behind him and there was more desert country ahead, but now the trail led through scattered tall pines where there was little undergrowth. Here and there boulders or rock outcrops could be seen through the trees.

It was late in the year and rather cold in the shade. But here and there he rode through patches of warm sunlight, and occasional meadows where nothing grew but brown grass and a few scattered pines. Good cattle country, but he saw no cattle.

Around a bend of the trail he caught sight of a wagon stopped in a little clearing. The middle-aged man with the lines in his hands turned a frank friendly face to smile at him and asked, "Where you bound, stranger?"

"Hell, I guess," Benton said before he noticed the two girls on the seat beside the man. He stopped the brown gelding and asked, "Trouble?"

"No, just lettin' the horses blow," the man said. "Been pushin' them right along. Want to get back to Rustler's Roost. I believe somebody named the town that as a bad joke. I took my wife to Santa Fe to see a doctor, but it was too late. She was a Mexican girl and her folks live there. They wanted her buried near her own people."

"Sorry," Jim Benton said, trying to hide a frown. Why did people tell him their troubles? He had no pity left to give.

"It was her idea to take the wagon and bring back a load of supplies," the man added, "and the girls wanted to go along, so we had to close our store in Rustler's Roost. That's why we're in a hurry to get back."

Benton took a closer look at the girls. Both had dark hair and eyes, but one had a smooth white face and the other's face was as brown as that of an Indian girl. Benton would never have guessed that she was half white, nor would he have been certain that the other girl was half Mexican. Both appeared to be around eighteen or nineteen. He had no idea which one was older.

"I'm Charlie Fry," the man said. "These are my girls, Rita and Nita." He grinned. "They ain't quite twins, but they only missed it by eleven months."

"Jim Benton," Benton said. He thought it unlikely that anyone in this area had heard of him.

It was obvious that Rita and Nita Fry had not, and just as obvious that they had no wish to get acquainted. The one with the clear white skin, whom he took to be Rita, gave him a cool glance. The other one did not even bother to glance at him.

Jim Benton touched the brim of his black hat and said dryly, "Nice meeting you." Then he touched the brown horse with his spurs and rode on along the trail.

"Maybe we'll see you in town," Charlie Fry called after him. "We should have the store open for business by tomorrow."

Benton rode on without replying or looking back.

The trail soon led him down out of the tall pines and wound among rocky hills dotted with stunted cedars. Below stretched the gray desert, and in the distance he caught a glimpse of a huddle of buildings that he took to be Rustler's Roost.

It was noon when he reached the one-street town. Most of the buildings were frame or log shacks with false fronts but here and there crouched a low-roofed adobe. The biggest adobe building said "FRY'S STORE" across the front. Riding past, Benton noticed the closed sign in the window.

Benton left his horse at the livery stable and walked back along the nearly deserted street with his saddlebags and blanket roll, turning into the two-story frame hotel, the Cedar House. It was the only hotel in town. He signed the register and paid a dollar for the first night. Going up to his room on the second floor, he dropped his saddlebags and blanket roll on the floor and glanced at the tall bleak-eyed stranger in the mirror, which showed him reversed, the holstered revolver on the left side.

Removing his hat and short close-fitting Mexican jacket, he rolled up his shirt sleeves, poured water from the pitcher into the basin on the washstand and washed his face and hands, drying with a towel. The clerk had told him that dinner was being served in the dining room. Going back down the stairs, he entered the dining room and ate at a table by himself in the corner, his back to the wall, ignoring the other diners who watched him with covert interest.

In the barbershop later, he got a shave and a hair trim and soaked a while in the barber's tub in the back room, then put on the clean clothes he had brought with him. They looked just like the clothes he had taken off, which he left at a Chinese laundry on his way back to the hotel.

In his room, he hung his hat and gun belt on the back of a chair and stretched out on the bed with his hands clasped behind his head, staring at the ceiling with still gray eyes.

He found himself thinking about the two girls he had seen on the wagon, Rita and Nita Fry. Rita's smooth white face had a rare, flawless beauty. But the other girl, though not quite as pretty, appeared to have a better figure, though not by much. They were both fine-looking girls, and all too well aware of it, Benton thought. From their quiet reserve and superior indifference he would never have guessed that they were the daughters of a friendly and talkative man like Charlie Fry. They did not resemble him in any way either.

Benton was tired from long riding and after a while he fell asleep. He was awakened late in the day by the sound of yells, hoofbeats and gunshots. Rising, he went to the window to look out.

Four or five riders were galloping their horses back and forth along the dusty street, whooping and firing their pistols into the air. A bunch of wild young cowhands letting off steam, he decided.

But Benton's attention was drawn to an older man, a big man pushing forty with a strong weathered face and graying hair, who seemed to be with the others but taking no part in the fun. He quietly rode his horse to a saloon across the street, swung down rather stiffly, tied the animal and pushed in through the swing doors.

When the others tired of their sport they also headed for the saloon, laughing as they went in and slapping one another on the back.

Jim Benton's eyes were uneasy as he turned away from the window. It was usually the wild young ones like that who caused him trouble. Older men like that big quiet fellow had learned that it was better to avoid trouble. But some never learned. Some did not live long enough.

Benton thoughtfully buckled on his cartridge belt, drew the gun from the holster and checked it. The gun was a .44 Frontier Colt with a five-and-a-half inch barrel and a plain walnut butt. Benton did not wear the gun for show.

Slipping the gun back into the holster, he put on his black hat and a dark gray wool coat that was warmer than his thin charro jacket. Also, he did not want to be mistaken for a Mexican or a Mexican lover. This was evidently a gringo town and there was no point in asking for trouble.

As he went down the stairs he again thought of Rita and Nita Fry. He doubted if girls as pretty as those two would be rejected because they were part Mexican, especially in a country where there were so few girls of any kind.

They did not start serving supper in the dining room until six, so Benton left the hotel and crossed to a restaurant. There was no one in sight, but he heard someone moving around in back. He sat down at a table against the wall where he could see the door and the street through the window.

It was several minutes before a tired-looking slender woman of about thirty came from the kitchen and looked at him curiously. "Hello," she said. "What would you like?"

"Anything you've got to eat and some black coffee."

"Beef stew and potatoes sound all right?"

"Sounds fine."

She went back into the kitchen.

A moment later the street door opened and three young men in their twenties came in. They were three of the ones Benton had seen a little earlier galloping their horses up and down the street and firing their guns in the air. They stared at him now with eyes that were half friendly and half challenging. But they went on to the counter and took stools without speaking to him.

The woman returned from the kitchen with Benton's supper and one of the men at the counter drawled, "Hello, Mary. That for me?"

She smiled. "No, but I can bring you some more for fifty cents."

"Sounds like my credit ain't good here no more."

"Not till you boys pay what you owe me."

"How much is that?"

"A little over thirty dollars. I've got it written down in back."

"Thirty dollars! That much?"

"Yep." She set Benton's food on the table before him and went back around behind the counter, studying the three young men. "If just one of you would work for a month, you'd have enough to pay your bill here."

All three of them chuckled at the notion of working for a month just to pay what they owed her. The tall shaggy-haired rider who had spoken before said, "We got our own place to keep up, Mary."

"But you're not keeping it up," she said in the same tired but patient tone as before. "If you're not in town you're off causing devilment somewhere else. You haven't got any stock and you haven't even fixed up that old shack you boys moved into."

"Who told you all that, Mary?"

"You think there are any secrets in a place like this?" she asked. "Everybody in the country knows about you boys, and they're keeping their eyes on you, waiting for you to get caught. I believe they named the town in your honor. It didn't have a name for a long time."

"Thanks for the warning," the talker drawled, while the other two chuckled. "I'll remember you said that when they put a rope around our necks. But right now I'm more worried about my belly. Couldn't you feed us just one more time, Mary? We'll pay you the next time we get any money."

"You said that the last time. And the time before that. I'd keep feeding you boys on credit if I could, but I can't. If business doesn't pick up, it looks like I may have to close the restaurant."

"I'd sure hate for you to do that, Mary. This is the only restaurant in town, and they won't give us no credit at the hotel."

One of the others, a heavyset young man with a swarthy round face, turned on his stool and regarded Benton with narrow eyes. "This stranger looks like he's rollin' in dough. He shouldn't mind loanin' us five or ten bucks."

Benton kept his attention on his food. "Sorry."

"What does that mean?"

"I don't imagine I'll be around when you get the money to pay me back."

The chunky man scowled. "What's five or ten bucks?"

"About a week's pay for a cowhand," Benton said. "If you need money you might consider going to work, like the lady suggested."

The third man swung around angrily. He was almost as tall as the shaggy-haired rider and almost as dark as the short one. He had slightly rounded shoulders, a hooked nose and bright piercing eyes. "We don't need no suggestions from you, mister," he said.

"No, all you need is my money," Benton said dryly.

Both the hook-nosed rider and the chunky one started to get to their feet, their fists clenched.

"Take it easy, Hawk," the shaggy-haired rider said in an uneasy tone. "You too, Chunk."

"I ain't in no mood for no lip from no fancy dude," Hawk said, but he sat back down. So did Chunk, after scowling at Benton in silence for a moment.

"I don't want any trouble here," the woman said. "I guess I'll feed you boys this time, but it will have to be the last time till you pay me. I've been getting supplies on credit at Fry's Store, but I hate to keep asking him for more credit till I pay my bill. And he lost his wife. That doctor in Santa Fe couldn't do anything for her. They got back a little while ago and stopped here to eat so the girls wouldn't have to cook."

The shaggy-haired rider grinned. "You mean they're back already? We'll have to mosey over after supper and see how Rita and Nita are doin'."

"Charlie said he wasn't going to open the store until tomorrow. But you might give them a hand unloading the supplies they brought back, if they haven't finished already."

The rider chuckled. "Looks like you aim to put us to work one way or another, don't it?"

"You boys should all go to work and settle down, before you get in bad trouble," she said. "But I don't guess it would be too easy to find a job now. All the ranches are laying men off for the winter, instead of hiring more."

She went into the kitchen, and Hawk grunted, "Who the hell wants a job?" He remembered Benton and turned to glare at him. "What do you work at?"

"I'm between jobs at the moment."

Hawk's sharp eyes pushed at him. "What sort of jobs?"

The shaggy-haired rider said without turning, "Take it easy, Hawk."

Hawk's face contorted with anger. "Don't tell me what to do, Pete. You ain't my boss. If I wanted a damned boss, I'd go to work."

"No, you wouldn't," Pete said. "You'd do anything to keep from goin' to work, just like me."

The chunky rider chuckled, and Hawk relaxed, turning as the woman came back with a plate of food in each hand.

"How much do I owe you, ma'am?" Benton asked.

"Fifty cents."

He laid a dollar on the table and rose.

"Wait," she said, "and I'll get your change."

"Forget it." He glanced at the three men sitting at the counter. "Just don't let anybody steal it."

Then he went out.

The preceding was from the gritty western novel
The Hellbound Man

To keep reading, click or go here:
http://amzn.to/1fTATJy

Excerpt from
Rebel With A Gun
by Van Holt

On a gray, drizzly day in the spring of 1865, a tall slender young man on a brown horse rode along the muddy street of Hayville, Missouri. Several heads turned to stare at him, but he seemed not to notice anyone, and he did not stop in the town, but rode on out to a weather-beaten, deserted-looking house and dismounted in the weed-grown yard.

At the edge of the yard there was a grave surrounded by a low picket fence and he went that way and stood with his head bared in the slow drizzle and stared at the grave with bleak, bitter blue eyes. He was only nineteen but looked thirty. He had been only fifteen when the war started. That seemed like a lifetime ago, another world —a world that had been destroyed. All that was left was a deserted battlefield, a devastated wasteland swarming with scavengers and pillagers.

An old black man with only one eye appeared from a dripping pine thicket and slowly reached up to remove a battered hat and scratch the white fuzz on his head.

"Dat you, Mistuh Ben?"

"It's me, Mose," Ben Tatum said.

"I knowed sooner or later you'd come back to see yo' ma's grave. She died two years back now. Never was the same aftuh we heard the news about yo' pa. And too she was worried sick about you. Is it true you rode with Quantrill, Mistuh Ben?"

"You can hear anything, Mose."

"Yessuh, dat's de truth, it sho' is. But I wouldn't rightly blame you if you did. Dem Yankees sho' did raise hell, didn't they, Mistuh Ben?"

Old Mose was something of a diplomat. Had he been talking to a Yankee, he would have said it was the Rebels who had raised hell.

Or he might have said it was Quantrill's raiders.

"The war's over, Mose."

"Yessuh, I sho' do hope so, I sho' do." Old Mose reached up and rubbed his good eye, and for a moment his blind eye seemed to peer at the tall young man in the old coat. "But folks say there's some who still ain't surrendered and don't plan to. I hear there ain't no amnesty for Quantrill's men. Is dat true, Mistuh Ben?"

"That's what I heard, Mose."

"Dat sho' is too bad. I guess dat mean there still be ridin' and shootin' and burnin' just like befo'."

"Maybe not, Mose."

"I sho' do hope not. Has you only got one gun, Mistuh Ben? I hear some of Quantrill's men carry fo' or five all at one time."

Ben Tatum glanced down at the double-action Cooper Navy revolver in his waistband. He buttoned his coat over the gun. "I just got in the habit of carrying this one, Mose. I wouldn't feel right without it."

"Guess a man can't be too careful dese days." Old Mose thoughtfully rubbed the wide bridge of his nose, his good eye wandering off down the road toward Hayville. "Well, I just come by to check on yo' ma's grave. She sho' was a fine woman. Mistuh Snyder down to de bank own de place now. I guess you heard his boy Cal done gone and married dat Farmer girl you was sweet on?"

Ben Tatum let out a long sigh. "No, I hadn't heard, Mose. But it doesn't matter now. I can't stay here."

Old Mose looked like he had lost his only friend. "Where will you go, Mistuh Ben?"

"I don't know yet. West, maybe."

He turned and looked at the old house with its warped shingles and staring, broken windows. He did not go inside. He knew the house would be as empty as he felt.

He turned toward his horse.

"Oh, Mistuh Ben!"

"What is it, Mose?"

"I almost forgot," old Mose said, limping forward. "Yo' ma's sister, what live over to Alder Creek, she said if I ever saw you again to be sho' and tell you to come by and see her."

"All right, Mose. Thanks."

He thoughtfully reached into a pocket, found a coin and tossed it to the old Negro.

A gnarled black hand shot up and plucked the coin out of the air. "Thanks, Mistuh Ben. I sho' do 'preciate it. Times sho' is hard since they went and freed us darkies. Them Yankees freed us but they don't feed us."

He rode back through Hayville. The small town seemed all but deserted. But it had always seemed deserted on rainy days, and sometimes even on sunny days. But for some reason Ben Tatum could no longer recall very many sunny days. They had faded into the mist of time, the dark horror of war.

He stopped at a store to get a few supplies. The sad-eyed old man behind the counter seemed not to recognize him. But Ben Tatum had been only a boy when he had left, and now he was a tall young man with shaggy brown hair and a short beard. He had not shaved on purpose because he had no wish to be recognized. And he suspected that old man Hill did not recognize him on purpose. It was usually best not to recognize men who had ridden with Quantrill.

The slow rain had stopped, and when he left the store Ben Tatum saw a few people stirring about. A handsome, well-dressed young couple were going along the opposite walk. The young man had wavy dark hair and long sideburns, a neatly trimmed mustache. He wore a dark suit and carried a cane, like a dandy, and his arrogant face was familiar. The girl had long dark hair and just a hint of freckles. It was Jane Farmer. Only it would be Jane Snyder now. Cal Snyder had stayed here and courted her and married her while Ben Tatum was dodging bullets and sleeping out in the wet and cold, when he got a chance to sleep at all. Cal Snyder had not gone to the war. His father had hired a man to go in his place, a man who had not come back. He had been killed at Shiloh.

Ben Tatum stopped and stared at her as if a mule had kicked him in the belly. But neither Jane Snyder nor her dandified husband showed the slightest sign that they recognized him or even saw him. They went on along the walk and turned into the restaurant.

With a sick hollow feeling inside him, Ben Tatum got back in his wet saddle and rode on along the muddy street, returning to the bleak empty world from which he had come, homeless now and a wanderer forever. The war had taught him how to lose. Turn your back and ride off as if it did not matter. Never let the winners know you cared.

"Ben! Ben Tatum!"

For a fleeting moment hope rose up in him like an old dream returning. But then he realized that it was not her voice, and when he looked around he saw a fresh-faced girl just blooming into womanhood, a girl with long light brown hair that was almost yellow and a face that looked somehow familiar. She was smiling and radiant and seemed happy to see him. Puzzled, he searched his memory but failed to place her, and it made him uneasy. He lived in a world where it did not pay to trust your closest friends, much less strange beautiful girls who seemed too happy to see you. Many girls that age had been spies during the war and had lured many a dazzled man to their destruction. Some of them might still be luring men to their destruction, for the war still was not over for some men and never would be over. Men like Ben Tatum. And the fact that she knew his name proved nothing.

So he merely touched his hat and kept his horse at the same weary trot along the muddy street, and behind him he heard a little exclamation: "Well!" He rode on out of town, wondering who she was. He noticed that it had started raining again.

Alder Creek was a two-day ride west of Hayville. There were no streets in Alder Creek, just narrow roads that wound among the trees that grew everywhere, and most of the houses were scattered about in clearings that had been hacked out of the trees and brush.

Ben Tatum's aunt lived in a big old house on a shelf above the hidden murmuring creek that had given the town its name. Her husband had died years ago in a mysterious hunting accident and she had soon remarried and had a lively stepdaughter. Her two sons had died in the war and she had no other children of her own.

Cora Wilburn had been a slender, attractive woman in her late thirties the last time Ben Tatum had seen her. But the war had aged her as it had aged everyone else. There were lines in her tired face and streaks of gray in her hair, and she had put on weight. But she seemed glad to see him, and it was good to see a smiling, friendly face.

She hugged him and patted his back just the way his own mother would have done had she lived to see him come home. "My, you've sure grown into a tall, fine-looking man," she said, blinking away tears. Her voice sounded as old and tired as she looked. "But you need a haircut and some decent clothes. Sam's a pretty good barber, they tell me, and you can have some of Dave's clothes. He was tall like you. I appreciate the nice letter you sent me when Dave and Lot were killed."

He nodded, and just then he noticed a tall slender girl of about thirteen standing on the porch watching him with lively green eyes and a mischievous smile. "This can't be Kittie," he said in a slow surprise.

"Yes, that's Kittie," Cora Wilburn said in her tired voice. "Ain't she run up like a weed? Soon be grown. It's getting hard to keep the boys away from her or her away from the boys."

Kittie Wilburn gave her dark head a little toss and flashed her white teeth in a smile, but said nothing.

"Sam's at the barbershop," Cora Wilburn added. "Soon as you eat a bite and catch your breath, you should go on down there and get some of that hair cut off your head and face. I want to see what you look like without that beard."

Sam Wilburn was a strange, moody man, by turns silent and talkative. He had a habit of watching you out of the corners of cold green eyes, without ever facing you directly. He was trimming an old man's white hair when Ben Tatum opened the door of the small barbershop. He glanced up at him out of those strange green eyes and said, "Have a seat. I'll be with you in a few minutes."

Ben Tatum sat down in a chair against the wall and picked up an old newspaper. The war was still going on when the newspaper was printed, but Quantrill had already disappeared and was thought dead by them and his followers had scattered, some of them forming small guerrilla bands of their own, or degenerating into common outlaws and looters, preying on the South as well as the North. Others had gone into hiding or left the country. Few had any homes left to return to, even if it had been safe to go home.

When the old man left, Ben Tatum took his place in the barber's chair and Sam Wilburn went to work on his hair. He did not seem very happy to see the younger man. They had never had much use for each other, and now and then Ben Tatum had idly wondered if Sam Wilburn had arranged the hunting accident that had left Cora Medlow an attractive young widow. Why Cora had married Sam Wilburn was another mystery he still had not figured out. But the world was full of things he would probably never understand.

Sam Wilburn glanced through the window at a wagon creaking down the crooked, stump-dotted road that passed for the town's main street. "I've been wondering when you'd show up," he said. When Ben Tatum made no reply, he asked, "You been to the house?"

Ben Tatum grunted in the affirmative.

Sam Wilburn worked in silence for a time, evidently doing a thorough job of it. The coarse brown hair fell on the apron in chunk's. Scattered among the brown, there were hairs that looked like copper wires, and there were more of them in his beard, especially on his chin. Those dark reddish copper hairs gleamed in his hair and short beard.

"What do you plan to do, now that the war's over?" Wilburn asked, his attention on his work.

"I ain't decided yet."

"You can't stay around here. They'll be looking for you."

Ben Tatum sighed, but said nothing. He sighed because he knew Sam Wilburn did not want him to stay around here. He had known already that they would be looking for him.

"Texas," Sam Wilburn said. "That's your best bet. I've been thinking about going down there myself. I don't think I'll like it much around here when the carpetbaggers move in. I don't like nobody telling me what to do or how to run my business."

"I doubt if it will be much better in Texas."

"Can't be any worse. Quite a few others around here and Hayville feel the same way. They've been talking about getting up a whole wagon train and going down there."

"I imagine talk about it is about all they'll ever do."

"No, they're serious. Even old Gip Snyder is talking about going. He says it's a new country with a lot of opportunities and we can build ourselves a new town down there where nobody won't bother us. Course, he plans to start a new bank, and I could start a new barbershop. The more I think about it, the better I like the idea."

"There'll be carpetbaggers in Texas just like there are here," Ben Tatum said.

"It won't be as bad. This state's been torn apart worse by the war than any other state in the country, and now that it's safe the carpetbaggers will be flocking in like vultures to pick our bones. Our money's already worthless. That's why old Gip Snyder is so keen on going. His bank at Hayville is in trouble, and he wants to salvage what he can and get out."

Ben Tatum shifted uncomfortably in the chair. "What about all the property he owns around Hayville?"

"I think he's found a buyer for most of it. That's the only thing that worries me. I don't know what I'd do with our property here if I went, and Cora ain't too keen on going. She's been in bad health lately. Losing them boys nearly killed her."

Ben Tatum was silent.

After a moment Wilburn asked, "What about the beard?"

"Get rid of it, I guess. Aunt Cora don't seem to like it."

After supper Ben Tatum went for a walk down along the creek. A path led him past an old shack almost hidden in the trees and brush. There was a light burning in the shack and through the window he caught a glimpse of a very shapely, blond-haired woman taking a bath. The long hair looked familiar.

When he got back to the Wilburn house he found Kittie in his room. "What are you doing here?" he asked, taking off the coat Aunt Cora had given him. It had belonged to Dave Medlow but it fitted Ben Tatum all right.

Kittie's lips curled back from her white teeth in a teasing smile. "Straightening up your room, Cousin Ben," she said with a deliberately exaggerated southern drawl.

"You run along," he said. "I'm not your cousin and the room don't need straightening up."

"That's right, we ain't cousins, are we?" she said. "We ain't no kin a'tall, now I think about it. But I was gonna marry you anyway. You sure do look handsome without that old beard. It made you look like a old man of about thirty."

"I'll be thirty before you're dry behind the ears," he said. He hung the coat in the closet and put his gun in a bureau drawer. In the mirror he saw Kittie Wilburn watching him with a smile, and he turned around with a frown. "Are you still here?"

"No, I'm still leaving. I just ain't got very far yet." She lay down on the bed and put her bare feet up on the gray wallpaper, so that her skirt fell down around her thighs, revealing very shapely legs for a skinny, thirteen-year-old girl. "Did you go see Rose?" she asked.

"Who?"

"Rose Harper. That girl who lives down by the creek. She just got back from Hayville a little while ago. I saw her go by. She lives over here now. Ever since she married Joe Harper. But she don't stay here much, 'cause he ain't never around. The bluebellies and nearly everybody else is looking for him, 'cause he rode with Quantrill. Like you."

"What does she look like?"

"Don't you know? You went to see her, didn't you? Anyway, you used to know her when she lived at Hayville with her folks."

"Wait a minute," Ben Tatum said. "Didn't Joe Harper marry that Hickey girl? Rose Hickey?"

"He shore did, Cousin Ben. He shore did."

"I thought that was what he told me after he came home the last time. My God, she was just a kid the last time I saw her."

"She ain't no kid now."

"She sure ain't," Ben Tatum agreed. "I saw her in Hayville and didn't even recognize her."

"I hate her," Kittie Wilburn said. "She makes me look plumb scrawny." She pulled her skirt up a little higher and looked at her thighs. "Do you think I'll ever outgrow it, Cousin Ben? Looking so scrawny and all?"

"You might," he said, "if I don't get mad and wring your neck."

"Oh, all right. I'll go." She swung her bare feet to the floor and rose, stretching and making a sort of groaning sound in her throat. She looked at him with that teasing smile. "But you've got to promise me something first."

"What?"

"I'll have to whisper it. I don't want anyone else to hear." She put her arms around his neck and rose on tiptoes, putting her warm moist lips close to his ear and whispering, "You've got to promise to marry me someday. Then I'll go."

"That'll be the day!"

She giggled and again made as if to whisper something, but this time she bit his ear and then ran from the room. At the door she pulled her skirt up to her waist, bent over and showed him her bottom. And it was quite a bottom for a skinny, thirteen-year-old girl to be flashing. He saw it in his mind until he went to sleep, and he wondered if he was the only one who had seen it. If so, it was probably only because she had not had an opportunity to show it to anyone else.

He knew he should tell Aunt Cora about the girl's naughty behavior, for her own good. But he also knew that he wouldn't, for his own good. Aunt Cora might think he had encouraged the child in some way, and think less of him because of it.

He slept late the next morning, and was awakened by the slamming of the door when Sam Wilburn left for the barbershop. He had just gotten dressed when he heard a dozen or more horsemen crowding into the yard, ordering all those inside to come out with their hands in the air.

The preceding was from the western novel
Rebel With A Gun

To keep reading, click or go here:
Coming Soon!

Excerpt from
A Few Dead Men
by Van Holt

The two men met on the trail, strangers with only one thing in common—they happened to be going in the same direction.

They did have one other thing in common, a deadly skill with firearms, but they did not discuss that at the time, though each was curious about the other.

Ben Cobbett would never see thirty again. Joe Deegan would never see thirty at all.

Cobbett was a tall lean man with pale hair, bleak gray eyes and a weathered brown face that might have been carved from solid rock. He wore a dust-colored hat, a faded corduroy coat, gray trousers, and a walnut-butted Colt .45 on his right hip.

Joe Deegan was about two inches shorter, five ten or a little better. He had rich dark chestnut hair, laughing blue eyes and a smooth round baby face that made him look younger than his actual age of twenty-five. He wore a black hat, black leather vest, blue shirt, black trousers and a black gun belt, with the holster and ivory-handled Colt .44 on the left side. He also rode a beautiful black horse that Cobbett suspected was stolen. Cobbett's own gelding was a rangy sorrel, and he had a bill of sale in his saddlebag.

As it was getting late, the two men decided to camp for the night beside a little stream near the trail. They took care of the horses first, then boiled coffee, cooked bacon and beans and pan bread. It was fall in the high desert country, warm days, cold nights, and the fire felt good. The hot coffee was fine also, and Cobbett sipped a second cup while Deegan finished the beans and bacon.

Deegan studied Cobbett with his smiling blue eyes. The younger man, not yet saddened by age or experience, seemed to find everything mildly amusing—even the bleak humorless face of Ben Cobbett and the high-peaked Montana hat he wore. Or perhaps it was Cobbett's neatly trimmed mustache that was a lot darker than his hair.

"You from Montana?" Deegan asked.

"I was there a few years," Cobbett said quietly. In keeping with western tradition he had not asked any questions himself, would not ask any.

Joe Deegan laughed quietly at the older man's taciturnity, his blank-faced disapproval of the question. Deegan was a young man and he did not have much regard for customs he considered out-of-date, especially as lawmen had never hesitated to break tradition and question him. He had little doubt that Cobbett had worn a badge at one time or another. He looked like the type—Deegan often bragged that he could spot a lawman a mile away.

Deegan drank his coffee thoughtfully, a hint of malice in his grin. He reflected that many ex-lawmen, without their badge to shield them, became sensitive and secretive about their former occupation. And well they might, for there were a lot of men around who would jump at a chance to fill them full of holes. Deep down nobody had much use for a lawman. Outlaws were a lot more popular.

"What were you back in Montana?" Deegan asked finally. "Lawman?"

"For a while," Cobbett answered shortly.

"I figgered you were," Deegan said. "I can always spot a lawman. Something different about them."

"I'm not a lawman anymore."

Deegan showed his white teeth in a hard grin. "They'll try to pin a badge as you the minute you ride into Rockville. The last marshal has prob'ly been shot by now. They bury one about once a month."

Cobbett finished his coffee and laid the tin cup aside. His face seemed even harder in the flickering firelight. "I'm through wearing a badge," he said. "I figure it's time I tried something else."

"If you ever aim to, it is," Deegan agreed. He glanced at the pale hair under Cobbett's hat. "That hair gray, or has it always been like that?"

"Might be a little gray in it. Seems to be getting lighter anyway."

Deegan chuckled. "Well, I guess everybody gets old sometime."

Cobbett's cold gray eyes narrowed a little. "Yeah, if they live long enough."

"How old are you anyway, Cobbett?" Deegan asked.

"Thirty-four."

Deegan's surprise showed. "Hell, I figgered you were closer to forty."

"Lot of people figgered that," Cobbett grunted. "I believe I'll turn in. Old man like me needs his rest."

"I think I'll ride on to Rockville," Joe Deegan decided. "It's only a couple more hours, and the boys are more likely to be in town at night. I ain't seen them for a while."

"Suit yourself." Cobbett was already spreading his blankets.

Deegan looked at him for a moment, then shivered and glanced at the sky. "You gonna get wet," he said. "I think it's gonna rain."

"I've been wet before."

Rockville was a one-street town of false-fronted frame buildings, surrounded on three sides by boulder-strewn hills and sagebrush. Just east of the town there was a stream in wet weather, a dry wash at other times. Once a few cottonwood trees had grown along the wash, but there were none left near the town. They had been used for lumber and firewood.

To Joe Deegan the place looked as if it had shriveled up and died. He had only been gone a few weeks, but evidently his memory had already started playing tricks on him. He had remembered a wide street filled with people on foot scrambling to get out of the way of wild riders galloping into town and firing their guns into the air. And on either side bigger buildings, mostly saloons and gambling halls, brightly lit with chandeliers and glowing in the dark, and noisy with the clink of chips, the tinkle of glass, the jingle of spurs, and the laughter of girls in gaudy low-cut dresses. But there was none of that. At ten o'clock the town was dark and quiet and almost deserted, with dim lights showing in only a few buildings and half a dozen horses tied in front of a saloon.

Toward the saloon Joe Deegan drifted, his face lighting up when he recognized the horses. He swung down at the rail, tied the black, and went in through the swing doors, spurs jingling, a reckless carefree smile on his round baby face. It was good to be back, even better when he saw the five men at the bar turn and start grinning from ear to ear. They were his pals, the fun-loving, work-hating boys he rode and rustled with. Even the bartender's bulldog face cracked in a grin. Even old Duffy Shaw, who had a heart like stone, was glad to see him back, and it was always good to see a friendly face, even one like Duffy's.

"I'll be a suck-egg mule!" Barney Nash roared. "If it ain't Joe Deegan, in the livin' flesh!"

The others greeted Deegan as he stepped up to the bar beside Nash and ordered a whiskey. Nash was a rock-hard heavyset bruiser wearing a small derby on his huge head, a tacky green coat and a red shirt that hung outside his striped trousers. By now he had killed at least a bottle by himself and his dark-stubbled red face had a bloated look. His mean little eyes were bloodshot and bleary and there was a kind of challenge in them, in spite of his show of friendliness. He had long suspected Deegan of trying to take his gang away from him, replace him as the leader, and he probably wasn't as happy to see the baby-faced killer back as he pretended.

"How was Cheyenne?" Barney asked, his voice a natural roar.

Deegan rolled and licked and lit a cigarette. "I didn't go to Cheyenne."

"You didn't?" Barney asked. "You said you was!"

Deegan glanced at the heavyset man, his blue eyes cold under slightly raised dark brows. "I changed my mind."

"Where the hell did you go?"

"Salt Lake."

"Salt Lake!" Barney Nash exclaimed. "What the hell did you go there for? Ain't nothin' there but a bunch of wife-beatin' Mormons."

Joe Deegan chuckled. "Then they must do a lot of beating, 'cause they sure got lots of wives."

Some of the boys laughed at that, and Chuck Moser, a big-toothed, pop-eyed young man, asked, "What was it like in Salt Lake, Joe?"

"Dead," Joe Deegan said. "Dead as this place." Then he squinted through his cigarette smoke and asked, "You boys been up to anything while I was gone?"

"Nothin' 'cept the usual," Barney Nash said, and a couple of the others chuckled. "Pickin's is gettin' slim and the competition tougher."

"The Pasco boys still acting tough?"

"'Bout like usual," Barney Nash said. Then he looked at Joe Deegan with a malicious grin. "They said if you ever come back around here they was gonna have you for breakfast."

Joe Deegan's blue eyes were narrow and cold under raised brows. "They better bring plenty of help."

Barney Nash spread his hamlike hands, watching Deegan with his mean little eyes. "Leave me and the boys out of it," he said. "It ain't our fight. It's between you and them. You got them sore foolin' around with Molly."

"They still better bring plenty of help," Joe Deegan said.

It was raining the next morning when Ben Cobbett rode into town. He left his horse at the livery stable, tramped through the mud with his saddlebags, blanket roll and Winchester and turned into the town's only hotel, brushing rain from his slicker and cleaning his boots as best he could before entering. At the desk he signed the register, climbed the stairs and cleaned up in his room.

He cleaned his guns, the Colt and the Winchester.

When the rain slacked off to a slow drizzle he left the hotel and crossed the mud to a restaurant for a late breakfast.

Just as he was finishing his bacon and eggs Joe Deegan came in with a cheerful grin. He sat down opposite Cobbett and laid his wet black hat on the table, running his fingers back through his wavy dark hair. "Saw you ride in," he said. "How you like our little town?"

Just then the waitress, who had barely spoken to Cobbett, came from the kitchen with a big smile and said, "Joe! When did you get back?"

"Last night," Deegan said, laughing quietly at her surprise.

"And you ain't even been in to say hello!" the waitress said. She was a rather pretty but tired-faced woman who appeared to be in her late twenties. She might have been either younger or older, for the dry climate had already gone to work on her face, making it hard to guess at her exact age.

Joe Deegan was still chuckling, pleased with the world, but pleased most of all with Joe Deegan. "It was raining too hard," he said. "Jane, this here is Ben Cobbett. He used to be a lawman back in Montana. Jane Keller, Ben."

Jane Keller glanced sharply at Cobbett, then looked at Joe Deegan in surprise. "He's a friend of yours?"

Deegan glanced at Cobbett and showed his white teeth in a generous smile. "Sure," he said and shrugged. "Everybody's my friend, Jane. You know that."

Jane Keller's sun-cured face was serious and her green eyes were worried. "I don't know," she said. "George and Dave Pasco say they ran you out of town and you better not ever come back."

Joe Deegan's laughing baby blue eyes suddenly narrowed and turned cold. But he quickly erased that expression and said easily, "Them boys just enjoy hearing theirselves talk. They didn't mean no harm."

"You're only saying that, Joe. Everybody knows they've got it in for you." Then she said, "Molly Hicks was in town the other day."

Joe Deegan's eyes brightened with interest. "She pretty as ever?"

The waitress pursed her lips. "She's pretty all right," she said in a way that seemed to leave a lot unsaid. "What can I bring you, Joe?"

"A big platter of steak and potatoes and about a gallon of black coffee," Deegan said cheerfully.

She glanced at Cobbett's cup. "Can I get you anything else? How about some more coffee?"

"You could fill it back up."

Joe Deegan chuckled and winked at the waitress. "A man of few words."

About to turn away, the waitress raised her brows as if she thought even those few would be better left unsaid. She looked suspiciously at the former lawman, then smiled at Joe Deegan, a known rustler and horse thief. Cobbett had heard about the baby-faced outlaw even before meeting him on the trail yesterday.

The waitress went into the kitchen and returned with the coffeepot and a cup for Deegan. She filled both cups, then paused beside Deegan's chair, glancing down at him. "Are your friends still in town? I heard them making noise down at Duffy Shaw's saloon last night."

Deegan grinned. "I left them sleeping it off on the saloon floor. That's where I spent the night myself, as a matter of fact."

"I wish you wouldn't hang around with that bunch, Joe," Jane Keller said. "They're going to get you in bad trouble one of these days. I know you ride with them just for the fun and excitement, but they're no good, Joe. A bad lot, all of them, and Barney Nash is worse than the others. He'd cut his own mother's throat just for the fun of it." Then she glanced uneasily at Cobbett, as if worried that she might have said too much.

Joe Deegan also looked at the ex-lawman, but he did not seem in the least worried. Rather he seemed to be enjoying himself. "They won't get me in no trouble," he said. "I'm more likely to get them in trouble."

"You shouldn't say things like that, Joe," Jane Keller said, again glancing at Cobbett. "I know you don't mean it, but others might get the wrong impression."

Deegan grinned. "You don't have to worry about Cobbett. He claims he's through being a lawman. But I figure somebody will try to pin a badge on him if he stays around here long."

The waitress gave Cobbett a guarded look. "Do you plan to stay in Rockville long, Mr. Cobbett?"

Cobbett was sitting back in his chair with his coffee, looking through the window with bleak eyes. It had started raining again. "Not long," he said.

The waitress looked relieved. She shifted her glanced back to Deegan and said with a smile, "I'll be right out with your breakfast, Joe. Would you settle for some bacon and eggs, like Mr. Cobbett had?"

Deegan shrugged, grinning his indifference. "Sure," he said, "If you'll throw in the hen."

Jane Keller smiled and went into the kitchen.

"Raining again," Joe Deegan said. "Looks like I'm gonna get wet yet." He smiled at Cobbett. "I can't stay in here long, or that girl would try to have me up before a preacher."

"You might do worse."

"She's more your type, Cobbett," Deegan said. "She'd start trying to reform me the first thing. She'd tell that preacher we'd be back in church on Sunday."

Cobbett did not say anything. His long weathered face was blank as if he had not been listening.

Joe Deegan regarded him with mild amusement. "You met the marshal yet? You two might hit it off."

"Not yet," Cobbett said.

"He don't leave his office much when it's rainy like this," Deegan said. "I was surprised we didn't have a new one by now, but one of the boys said it was still the same one, Tobe Langley. Maybe you've heard of him. Around here he's known as a bad man with a gun."

"The name doesn't ring a bell."

Deegan shrugged. "Well, Montana's a long ways from here. What brought you out this way anyhow, Cobbett?"

"Just riding," Cobbett said. "I've always had the feeling that if I kept on going, sooner or later I'd find what I'm looking for. It comes on me every two or three years and I quit whatever I'm doing and hit the trail again."

"What are you looking for?"

"Maybe that's the trouble," Cobbett said. "I don't know."

Joe Deegan chuckled. He seemed to find the tall quiet man more and more amusing. Perhaps not wanting Cobbett to leave and deprive him of entertainment, he said, "Maybe you should hang around here a while. You might find whatever you're looking for."

"I doubt that," Cobbett said. "I guess I'll push on when it quits raining and my horse gets a few days' rest."

The preceding was from the gritty western novel
A Few Dead Men

To keep reading, click or go here:
http://amzn.to/18Xu7ic

More hellbound gunslinging westerns by Van Holt:

A Few Dead Men
http://amzn.to/18Xu7ic

Blood in the Hills
http://amzn.to/16jWNvB

Brandon's Law
Coming Soon!

Curly Bill and Ringo
http://amzn.to/Z6AhSH

Dead Man Riding
http://amzn.to/1aknrFD

Dead Man's Trail
http://amzn.to/ZcPJ47

Death in Black Holsters
http://amzn.to/1aHxGcv

Dynamite Riders
http://amzn.to/ZyhHmg

Hellbound Express
http://amzn.to/11i3NcY

Hunt the Killers Down
http://amzn.to/Z7UHjD

Maben
Coming Soon!

Rebel With A Gun
Coming Soon!

Riding for Revenge
http://amzn.to/13gLILz

Rubeck's Raiders
http://amzn.to/14CDxwU

Shiloh Stark
http://amzn.to/12ZJxcV

Shoot to Kill
http://amzn.to/18zA1qm

Six-Gun Solution
http://amzn.to/10t3H3N

Six-Gun Serenade
http://amzn.to/164cS7t

Son of a Gunfighter
http://amzn.to/17QAzSp

The Antrim Guns
http://amzn.to/132I7jr

The Bounty Hunters
http://amzn.to/10gJQ6C

The Bushwhackers
http://amzn.to/13ln4JO

The Fortune Hunters
http://amzn.to/11i3VsO

The Gundowners
(formerly So, Long Stranger)
http://amzn.to/16c0I2J

The Gundown Trail
http://amzn.to/1g1jDNs

The Hellbound Man
http://amzn.to/1fTATJy

The Last of the Fighting Farrells
http://amzn.to/Z6AyVI

The Long Trail
http://amzn.to/137P9c8

The Man Called Bowdry
http://amzn.to/14LjpJa

The Stranger From Hell
http://amzn.to/12qVVqd

The Vultures
http://amzn.to/12bjeGl

Wild Country
http://amzn.to/147xUDq

Wild Desert Rose
http://amzn.to/XH7Y27

Brought to you by Three Knolls Publishing
Independent Publishing in the Digital Age

www.3knollspub.com

THREE KNOLLS PUBLISHING

About the Author:

Van Holt wrote his first western when he was in high school and sent it to a literary agent, who soon returned it, saying it was too long but he would try to sell it if Holt would cut out 16,000 words. Young Holt couldn't bear to cut out any of his perfect western, so he threw it away and started writing another one.

A draft notice interrupted his plans to become the next Zane Grey or Louis L'Amour. A tour of duty as an MP stationed in South Korea was pretty much the usual MP stuff except for the time he nabbed a North Korean spy and had to talk the dimwitted desk sergeant out of letting the guy go. A briefcase stuffed with drawings of U.S. aircraft and the like only caused the overstuffed lifer behind the counter to rub his fat face, blink his bewildered eyes, and start eating a big candy bar to console himself. Imagine Van Holt's surprise a few days later when he heard that same dumb sergeant telling a group of new admirers how he himself had caught the famous spy one day when he was on his way to the mess hall.

Holt says there hasn't been too much excitement since he got out of the army, unless you count the time he was attacked by two mean young punks and shot one of them in the big toe. Holt believes what we need is punk control, not gun control.

After traveling all over the West and Southwest in an aging Pontiac, Van Holt got tired of traveling the day he rolled into Tucson and he has been there ever since, still dreaming of becoming the next Zane Grey or Louis L'Amour when he grows up. Or maybe the next great mystery writer. He likes to write mysteries when he's not too busy writing westerns or eating Twinkies.

14470356R00070

Printed in Great Britain
by Amazon.co.uk, Ltd.,
Marston Gate.